My PUMPKIN

My Holiday Tails

Marina Simcoe

To my Captain

My Pumpkin

Chapter 1

Cassy, 10 years old

"I want this one!" I threw myself onto the biggest pumpkin at the stand. It was so huge, the farmer had it on the ground, not in the wagon with the rest of them.

Mom tapped my shoulder. "Cassy, baby, it won't even fit into our apartment."

She smiled apologetically at the man selling the pumpkins at the farmer's market in our part of the city. But I refused to let go. This was the biggest pumpkin I'd ever seen in my life. My arms didn't even come close to wrapping all the way around it.

I wanted it.

"I'll keep it in my room." I'd have to shove my bed all the way to the wall to make space for this thing, but it'd be totally worth it.

"Cassidy," mom's voice gained that stern note it always did when she called me by my full name. "We're not getting that one. We can't even lift it. How are we going to carry it back to our building? Choose another one."

The farmer grinned at me, gesturing at the wagon piled high with bright orange pumpkins. "I've got a whole wagon-full of them. See? Surely, you'll find one you like in here."

I briefly considered stomping my feet and maybe whining a little. It rarely helped me get my way. But if we were in public, Mom would give in sometimes just to keep me quiet.

By the look of her, however, it was unlikely to happen today. Mom had her arms crossed over her chest. Her dark-brown eyes narrowed.

And her lips were pinched into that unimpressed expression she had when I acted up.

"Fine." I gave up and climbed off the giant pumpkin, then shuffled over to the wagon filled with the smaller, far less impressive ones.

They were okay. Some were perfectly round, others had funny squished or elongated shapes. None looked good enough after that giant one, though.

Something twinkled deep inside the pile. An orange glow shone from the darkness between the orbs.

"Ooh, what's that?" Straining my barely there arm muscles, I rolled aside a couple of pumpkins to find the one that was glowing.

This one was small, even smaller than most. It'd easily fit into my room. I wouldn't even have to move the furniture around to accommodate it. It'd fit on my bookshelf. Or even on the windowsill.

"How about this one?" I presented it to my mom.

"I don't think it's a pumpkin, hun." She took it from me and turned it over in her hands.

The glow stopped when she took it. But I still liked it. It was smooth and just a little brighter orange than the rest.

"I want to get this one," I insisted.

Mom seemed doubtful.

"It looks plastic. You won't be able to carve it." She turned to the farmer. "What is it, actually?"

He rubbed the back of his neck.

"Not sure. I've no idea how it got there. Is it yours, Linda?" he asked the vendor to his left, a plump woman in a gorgeous sweater with black cats printed on it. She was selling home-made Halloween decorations.

"Nope." She shook her head. "It can't be one of mine. You must've brought it from the farm. It was buried all the way in your wagon."

If no one was selling it, then I found it. And finders were keepers, right? I wrapped my arms tightly around my new pumpkin.

Mom hesitated. "Maybe it's someone's toy? A kid lost it? We should take it to the lost-and-found."

"But it's not lost. It's mine," I protested.

The pumpkin glowed softly again. When I pressed it to my chest, I felt it pulse warmly. I smiled, already imagining it in my room. I didn't even need to put a candle inside it because it shone all on its own.

"Well, Linda may be right." The farmer scratched his chin. "It might've come from the farm with us. Though, I've no idea how it got to the farm, either."

"I want to buy it," I had to remind the grownups of the task at hand. Mom and I came here to buy a pumpkin for Halloween. And I'd chosen one.

Mom looked around. "Well, if it doesn't belong to anyone..."

"It belongs to me," I said resolutely. "Finders keepers."

The farmer laughed.

"That's fine. Just keep it." He waved his hand.

"How much is it?" Mom opened her purse.

The man shrugged. "I don't even know what to charge. It clearly didn't grow on my farm. Just take it."

Happy I got what I wanted after all, I left them to figure out the details between themselves. Hugging my pumpkin to my chest, I skipped to the stand nearby that sold skewers of whimsically decorated marshmallows. Mom always got me one of those when we came to the farmer's market right before Halloween. I loved coming here.

It was the best day ever.

A year later.

I OPENED THE DOOR TO our apartment and hung my school bag on the hook by the door.

It was quiet. The apartment was empty. Mom worked long shifts at the hospital as a nurse. She wasn't coming home until much later that night. Dad wouldn't be back until the day after tomorrow. He worked as a pilot and was often gone for several days at a time.

When I was smaller, they'd tried to schedule their work shifts so that one of them was always home with me. Occasionally, when their schedules had overlapped despite their best efforts, they had hired our elderly neighbor to look after me.

Now that I was bigger and didn't need a babysitter, they didn't mind having their work shifts overlap. That way, we had more time to spend as a family when they both got days off at the same time.

I skipped down the hallway toward the kitchen to make myself a snack when a loud crash came from inside of the apartment. I froze.

Did we have an intruder? I backed up to the front door.

In case of an emergency, I had two options: either call nine-one-one or run downstairs and get the doorman, Mister Riley. Depending on the kind of emergency, of course, which wasn't always that easy to figure out, as I'd learned.

My face warmed up at the embarrassing memory of me running downstairs in my pajamas last spring because Mom and Dad weren't home and there was a funny noise coming from the bathroom. The noise as it had turned out was made by a bee caught in the shower curtain, not by a scary robot from outer space like I'd convinced myself to believe. Dad had laughed his head off when Mister Riley had told him that story. And Mom had told me that it was a good idea to think first about what an emergency meant.

"Sometimes," she'd said, "it wouldn't hurt to investigate a little on your own instead of panicking right away."

I stopped with my back to the front door, without opening it to run outside, and listened for the noise again.

No other suspicious sounds came. Maybe this wasn't an emergency, after all? What if something just fell off my desk, like a book or a toy? I'd look really stupid if I ran to Mister Riley again.

Mom was right, I had to *investigate*.

The noise appeared to have come from my bedroom. It was the first room up the hallway after the kitchen. I made a quick detour to the kitchen to grab a rolling pin just in case there *was* an intruder waiting for me in my room.

Holding the rolling pin in front of me, I padded to my bedroom door. Not a sound came from behind the door. I leaned closer and pressed my ear to it. Still, all seemed quiet. Maybe there hadn't been a noise at all, and I'd just imagined it?

Unless the intruder knew I was in the apartment and was waiting for me, very quietly.

I took a few deep breaths before placing a hand on the door handle and turning it. Holding the rolling pin ready, I cracked the door open.

My bed with the pink and orange bedspread came into view. Mom and I had cleaned my room just a day ago, so there weren't any piles of clothes or toys on the floor for an intruder to hide in.

The door to my closet was open, as it should be. I always had it open—less chance for closet monsters to sneak up on me undetected.

Thankfully, both the room and the closet looked empty and monster-free. The only place for the intruder to hide would be under my bed. But Mom stored boxes with my winter clothes under there. So, the intruder would have to be really short and skinny to fit into the space between the boxes.

Clutching the rolling pin in both hands, I entered the room, keeping an eye on the bed. The bright orange pieces of my pumpkin on the floor caught my eye, and I forgot all about the intruder.

"Oh no!" I tossed the rolling pin onto the bed and crouched by the broken pieces under the window.

This was my pumpkin, the one I'd gotten at the farmer's market last year. I'd kept it on my windowsill ever since. It was my favorite night-light. Its soft pulsing glow made me feel safe at night, even when Mom and Dad weren't home. And when I felt sad, I liked to cuddle with it. It always made me feel warm and fuzzy inside when I hugged it.

Now, it was broken. Three large chunks of the orange shell lay on the carpet. The outer side was smooth and glossy. The inside—the part I'd never seen before—happened to be white and soft, like a squishy marshmallow.

I picked up two of the pieces and tried to fit them together.

"Maybe Daddy can glue it back together?" I muttered under my breath.

Something scratched under the bed. The sound sent me up to my feet again. Grabbing the rolling pin, I jumped onto the bed.

"Who's there?" I tried to make my voice sound deep and scary. "Get out!"

There really wasn't that much space under my bed. The last time I'd crawled under there myself was to get a baseball that had rolled under there by accident. It happened months ago, and it'd been a tight fit between the boxes, even for me.

I adjusted my hands on the rolling pin. The fact that the intruder couldn't be much bigger than me felt encouraging.

A tapping sound came from under the bed. It moved from one end to the other and sounded very much like tiny footsteps. If it was an intruder, it would be the size of...a garden gnome? No one higher than that could actually *walk* under my bed. I leaned over the edge, feeling more confused than scared now.

Something orange crawled from under the bed. It looked round. Its color was the same bright shade as my pumpkin. Only instead of glossy and smooth, the thing was...fluffy.

"Hey," I called from the bed.

The thing turned around and blinked its long chocolate-brown eyelashes at me. It had two eyes—one blue, one green—with lighter dots pulsing inside them. Two pointy furry ears stood up. It also had a black button nose, four short paws, and two, yes *two*, tails that were so fluffy, they looked like two fuzzy pompoms attached to his chubby bum.

The creature looked like a toy. But it was most definitely alive.

"You're so stinking cute!" I squeaked, tossing aside the rolling pin.

The creature had clearly come from my pumpkin. Though, I wasn't entirely sure how that could've happened. I didn't really care, either. The thing was so fluffy, I just wanted to grab, pet, and squeeze it.

"Come here, you... Whatever the heck you are." I picked it up.

It snorted but didn't protest much. Its orange fur had some white in it, I discovered, upon a closer inspection. It was thicker around its neck, like a wide fur collar. Its feet were black, as if it was wearing socks. And it had the softest white belly I'd ever seen.

I scratched behind its ears, and the animal nuzzled into my elbow.

"You look like a puppy," I said uncertainly. "I'd never had a puppy before. I hope Mom will let me keep you."

Because I really, really wanted to keep him. Or *her*. Or *it*... Whatever it was.

Holding my new puppy in one arm, I grabbed my tablet and typed into the search bar *"kinds of dogs."* I had to figure out what kind I got. It wasn't always easy to tell with puppies, I'd heard.

"I think you might be a corgi," I determined after some research. The orange and white colors of my new dog fit that breed. As did the cute little face. "You're a bit fluffier than them. And shorter. And you have two tails. And black paws... Well, maybe you're not entirely a corgi. Maybe you're a mix with something else." Not that it really mattered, anyway. It was the cutest puppy I'd ever seen, and I loved it already.

Next, I researched what in our kitchen I could feed to the puppy since we didn't have any dog food in the house. The puppy refused to eat a raw egg but seemed happy with the ham and cheese sandwich I made for myself and then shared with it.

"I never had a pet," I told it. "But I always wanted one."

At night, I made a bed for the puppy in one of the drawers of the dresser in my room. Then I brushed my teeth and turned off the lights to go to bed.

My room looked different without the soft, warm glow of the pumpkin I'd gotten used to in the past year. The streetlights didn't have the same color. Their light was bluish and cold, making me think of ghosts or spaceships with aliens. The sound of traffic on the street below my window also kept me awake for some reason. Normally, I was used to it and even found it soothing. But not tonight.

A tiny squealing noise came from the dresser drawer.

"You can't sleep either?" I climbed off the bed and picked up the puppy. "Well, I guess you can sleep with me tonight."

I climbed back under the covers. The puppy was warm and fluffy. Its little heart thudded softly against my chest when I pressed its small, round body to me.

"Just for tonight, though, okay? Mom is not going to like it if she sees you in my bed..." I yawned, feeling comfy and warm. "I think I'll call you Pumpkin," I mumbled, drifting off to sleep.

"CASSY? WHAT IS THIS?" Mom stood in the kitchen, still wearing her scrubs.

When she'd come home after a long, late shift, she often was too tired to change. She'd just crash on the couch for a few hours. In the morning, she'd wake up to have breakfast with me and to take a shower. After I'd leave for school, she'd go to her bedroom to sleep, often until I came home in the afternoon.

That morning, I'd made us some bacon and scrambled eggs while she'd slept on the couch. It was her favorite breakfast. I hoped it'd put her in a good mood before she saw Pumpkin. But she hadn't even taken a bite before the silly puppy waddled out of my bedroom.

"I'm asking what this is?" She pointed at the round, fluffy thing.

I blew out a breath, hanging my head. "A puppy. I think."

Come to think of it, the creature didn't really look that much like a dog, more like a stuffed toy, or a cartoon character, or something.

"A puppy?" Mom stared at it. "Cassidy, where did you get a dog?"

She used my full name again. It was not a good sign.

I nervously tugged at one of my two dozen braids. "Well, funny thing... But I think it came from my pumpkin. The one I had on my window, remember? I came home from school yesterday, and the pumpkin was broken, and—"

She stopped my rambling by lifting a hand, then headed to the coffeemaker.

"I swear, Mom," I insisted. "The pumpkin must've hatched or something..."

"Right. And my head is about to crack open, too." She rubbed her forehead before starting the coffeemaker, then stared at Pumpkin, her hands on her hips. "He can't stay."

The puppy looked up at her, blinking innocently, then plopped down, sitting with his butt on my foot.

"But where else can he go?" I asked. Somehow, Pumpkin was now a "he."

Mom blew a lock of her chestnut hair away from her face. Her hair was wavy, not nearly as curly as mine. I got Dad's hair and skin color. But I had Mom's brown eyes. Dad's were much darker than hers or mine, almost black.

"The puppy has to go back to where he came from, Cassy," she said firmly. "He must belong to someone in the building. He probably wandered off into the hallway and snuck into our apartment when you opened the door. He's likely the one who knocked your pumpkin off the window, too, and broke it. He's trouble. We need to return him as soon as possible."

"But *where?*" I protested. "There are no missing dog posters in the building. No one is looking for him. He has nowhere else to go."

Mom leaned with her hip against the counter as the coffeemaker sputtered and brewed. "We'll have to speak with Mister Riley to see if someone is looking for a lost puppy."

"But if no one is, can we keep him?" I wouldn't give up hope.

She pursed her lips in that unimpressed expression of hers. Except that she also looked tired. Very tired. Long shifts at the hospital were hard.

"Cassy, we can't look after it," she said in a much softer voice.

Hope sparked brighter in me.

"But I can! I'll walk him first thing in the morning, before school. Then, I'll walk him again after school. And you know what? Pumpkin knows how to use the toilet, anyway."

"What are you talking about?" She got a cup from the cabinet and filled it with coffee. She always drank it black—no cream, no sugar.

"Yes, he does. He peed on the bathroom floor this morning. I cleaned it up with the toilet paper and flushed it. Then he climbed onto the seat and pooped into the toilet." I chatted, piling a plate high with bacon and eggs for her. She needed to eat. She always seemed to be in a better mood when she wasn't hungry.

"Thanks, baby." Mom took a fork I gave her and speared a slice of cucumber on it from the salad I'd made. "He pooped in the toilet? Are you sure? Dogs don't use toilets."

"Oh, yes, they do. The smart ones do. I've seen it in videos. I'll show you some. There's one where a dog even flushes the toilet after himself. I'm sure Pumpkin can learn how to flush, too. He's smart. He just needs to grow a little. Right now, he's too short to even reach the handle to flush."

Mom ate in silence for a little while, and I let her, afraid that if I talked too much, I'd irritate her. She was less likely to agree to anything if she was irritated.

"What will your dad say?" She sighed.

I tried to hide a smile as huge relief flushed over me. Dad was the least of my worries. If Mom said yes, he'd never say no.

"I need someone, Mom," I pleaded. "It'll be good to have Pumpkin around. You and Dad are never home."

Mom winced as if I'd slapped her.

"I mean, I'm not complaining," I added quickly.

I knew she wished she could spend more time with me. She worked so hard. And when she got home, she was often too tired and slept a lot. Dad was the same. We had lots of fun when the three of us went on vacations as a family. But most of the year, it was just me.

"I'm not allowed to have friends over when I'm home alone," I said. "I can't even open the door to anyone. But now, I won't be alone. I'll have Pumpkin."

With another deep sigh, she looked at the puppy again. He sniffed the floor around one of the legs of the kitchen table.

"Well, we're allowed a pet by the home association's rules. And he seems quiet. He hasn't barked yet."

"He doesn't bark," I rushed to assure her. "He just snorts and farts...a little."

She took a sip of her coffee, then rubbed her chin in thought. "We'll need to get a vet to look at him. He may have fleas or worms. And why the heck does he have two tails?"

I beamed. My Pumpkin was here to stay.

Chapter 2

Pumpkin

Ten years later.

"Aww, who's a good boy? Who's a good boy?" Cassy cooed.

He wasn't a boy, not a human boy, anyway. Though the vet confirmed him as a *possible* male. But Cassy was rubbing his belly, and he would never object to any signs of her attention. Rolling over to his back, he gave her more to rub.

"You're so cute. Just look at this fluffy fluff-fluff. Look at this spoiled little puppy." She grabbed his nose and kissed his forehead.

He wasn't a puppy, either. And he certainly wasn't little. In the past ten years, he'd grown much taller, he reached higher than Cassy's waist when he stood on all four feet. If he placed his front paws on her shoulders, he was way taller than her.

Overall, he knew what he *wasn't*. The question remained what he actually *was*?

He'd discovered early on that he could access the Internet remotely, without needing a device. It put the vast knowledge of humankind at his fingertips, figuratively speaking, of course, since he had no fingers, just paws.

After years of searching the web, he'd concluded he wasn't even a dog. What he was, however, he'd failed to identify. Some parts of him might look similar to those of a dog, a fox or even a wolf, but no species fit him perfectly.

The vet had seemed as confused as everyone else when Cassy and her mom had brought him to the clinic ten years ago. At the end, she'd just told Cassy and her mom that Pumpkin must have some birth defects and abnormalities. She'd said to "enjoy him while he lasts." She'd also advised Cassy's mom against doing any x-rays or tests since...well, he wasn't supposed to *last*, anyway, so there was no need to waste money.

But there he was, a decade later, feeling stronger and healthier than ever. Maybe a vet wasn't the right doctor for him after all?

"Ooh, guess what?" Cassy made her brown eyes wider, looking excited, as if she was about to tell him a secret. "Guess what we're going to do today, Pumpkin?" She took a pause, as if inviting him to take a guess.

He couldn't reply, of course, not with words. So, he lifted his three long tails—the third one grew a few years ago—and waved them in the air, similar to the way that dogs did.

It made her giggle. She always looked so happy when he did "normal dog things." That was the main reason he did them at all. Wagging his tails always made him feel silly, but he was rewarded with the sound of her giggles that made his skin tingle with pleasure under his fur.

"Oh, you know that, don't you? The smart puppy that you are? Of course you do. You know where we're going." She raked her fingers through the soft white fur on his belly. The pleasure kicked into a new gear. It was so intense, his hind legs jerked involuntarily.

"Who likes belly rubs? This big boy likes belly rubs," she continued to murmur utter nonsense which he didn't mind at all as long as she kept scratching his belly.

He'd always liked her pets and cuddles. Wrestling with her was fun too. Lately, however, his reaction to her touch had been turning into something else. It made him wish for more. For something...something he couldn't really name.

Despite her warnings on the night he'd first hatched, she had let him sleep in her bed again the next night, and the next... They had slept together every night since. Until her bed had become his, and no one even questioned his right to be in there with her anymore.

Cassy would fall asleep with her arms wrapped around him. When she lay next to him, he made a rhythmic thudding noise in his chest and increased his body temperature a little—both seemed to comfort her.

If she woke up at night after having a scary dream, she would bury her face into the fur on his neck and splay her hand on his chest, right over the part he made thud for her. Then, she would fall asleep again, breathing evenly.

A few nights ago, something else happened, however. Cassy woke up with a moan, not a whimper. The sound seemed to reach all the way through to his gut. Something he had no control over still pulsed low in his belly when he recalled that moan. She'd stared at his eyes for the longest moment, then...she kicked him out of her bed and out of her room.

That hurt. The unpleasant feeling from the unexplained rejection still scratched inside his chest. Thankfully, she'd let him back into her bed again the following night, and things seemed to be back to normal once again.

"That's right!" Cassy exclaimed excitedly. "We're going to the park."

She jumped up, waving her arms in the air in a severely exaggerated delight at her idea. He wagged his tails harder to match her enthusiasm. She clearly loved going to that park, and he absolutely didn't mind tagging along. As far as he was concerned, he didn't care *where* she took him as long as she stayed with him.

Since Cassy started college a few years ago, she had even less time to spend with him. She wanted to be a nurse, like her mom. He loved her focus and determination in that area and was proud of her. But he was also grateful that she hadn't moved out of her parents' place, like many college students did, and hadn't left him behind. That was the advantage of living in a big city—Cassy didn't have to leave to go to college. Her campus was just a short bus ride away.

"All right." She slapped his flank. "I'll go get changed quickly, then we'll leave. Okay?"

She jumped off the living room couch and skipped to her bedroom to change out of her pajamas.

He climbed off the couch, too, and stretched his back. Going to the park allowed him to run, which he was looking forward to. The need to move turned torturous if he stayed cooped up in the apartment for an entire day.

Cassy's phone rang inside her bedroom.

"Hi, Kat." She picked it up.

He turned his ears to catch more of their conversation. Kat was Cassy's friend from college. Through their phone calls and texts, he'd learned all about Cassy's life outside of the apartment. It worried him that she spent so much time out there, on her own and out of his sight. Listening in on her phone conversations was one of the ways he'd been keeping an eye on her and ensuring her safety the best he could.

Using nothing but his brain, he connected remotely to Cassy's phone to hear Kat's end of the conversation, too.

"So," Kat chatted. "I ran into Sasha in the gym this morning. Apparently, her roommate Donna dated that guy you made out with last night. What's his name? RJ?"

A low growl vibrated through his chest.

Cassy let a man touch her. Again? His hackles rose. The thought of a man's hands on Cassy's body made him inexplicably sick to his stomach. The kibbles he'd had for breakfast threatened to come up.

He searched her phone for the contact named "RJ," found it, and re-directed all calls and messages from that number directly to his own system.

"Oh... She did?" Cassy's voice faltered a little. "But they're not together anymore, are they?"

"No. She broke up with him because she'd caught him with Danielle."

"Caught them doing *what*, exactly?"

"Not sure. But obviously it was bad enough for her to break up with him."

A notification of an incoming message sounded in Pumpkin's head. It was a text for Cassy from the infamous RJ.

"Hi, beautiful. Slept well?"

He sounded like a sleazeball, Pumpkin decided, promptly deleting the message. Cassy didn't need to see this one. In fact, she didn't need to have anything to do with that RJ dude.

"That's too bad," she sighed. "He's such a good kisser."

The sleazeball had kissed her!

Pumpkin's stomach flipped and something unpleasant burned in his chest. Was he having indigestion? Maybe it was time for Cassy to change his kibbles. He should research dog food online. Maybe something organic would agree with him better?

Though, his favorite food was whatever Cassy shared with him after her classes. They'd often cuddle on the couch and watch TV together in the afternoon. She'd feed him half of her sandwich, or some pizza crust, or other equally delicious things. That was his favorite time of the day and his preferred type of food.

There were also quite a few recipes online he wished he could try. Though making any of them required hands he didn't have. Not much could be done with paws.

"Well, if RJ calls, I'll talk to him," Cassy said to Kat.

"You would? Are you sure?" Kat was a good friend, always looking out for Cassy.

"I mean, thanks for the info. But I'd like to get to know RJ a little better myself, instead of passing a judgment based on what someone said."

"True. Just be careful, okay?"

Cassy heaved a breath.

"With my luck, he probably won't call, anyway. No one ever does. It's like I meet someone, we have a great time together, and then...nothing. Not a call or a text. Ever. And when I try to contact them myself, they either don't answer or their phone number is suddenly not in service. Is there something so horribly wrong with me that no one wants to take me on a second date?"

Pumpkin dropped his head on his front paws. He hated to see Cassy unhappy. But why would he let her waste her time on some guy who wasn't good for her? And none of them were good enough for his Cassy.

Ever since that first one, the boy she dated in high school... Pumpkin had deleted his name from his memory a long time ago and had no desire to retrieve it ever again. That little prick had made Cassy cry.

He'd never forget her running into the apartment one evening, her eyes red and swollen, sobs tearing from her chest. She'd spent the entire night crying into the fur on his neck. He still shuddered, recalling her body shaking with sobs as she clung on to him.

Ever since then, Pumpkin vowed he would never let a man do that to her again. And it had worked. Cassy might be sad now, but she wasn't crying or heartbroken over another asshole, was she? And Pumpkin was determined to keep it that way.

"Honestly, I must be the only virgin left in college," she complained to Kat. "It's embarrassing. I'm twenty-one, for Pete's sake."

"Well, it's unusual," Kat agreed. "But lots of guys are into that *first-time* thing. Don't worry, Cass, you'll find one to pop your cherry soon enough."

"Not on my watch," Pumpkin scoffed inwardly and moved RJ's number into the folder of *Dead Contacts,* where it was to remain from now on as good as buried.

Cassy was beautiful, smart, and kind. Her smile made him warm and tingly all over, and her laughter was the best sound in the world. He didn't care who this RJ dude was; RJ didn't deserve her. None of them did.

"Well, I was about to go for a jog with Pumpkin when you called, Kat. I'd better go if I want to have enough time to make the full loop around the park."

Cassy hung up. A few minutes later, she exited her bedroom. Her tight curls were pulled up into a high, round ponytail that looked like a bun on the top of her head. Dressed in a pair of tight leggings and a bright yellow sports bra, she took his breath away.

Somehow, over the years, Cassy had grown from the skinny little kid with knobby knees and elbows into this gorgeous woman. Protecting her from every possible danger, including the attention of all those obnoxious men, grew harder by the minute. It was a full-time job by now, but someone had to do it. And Pumpkin viewed it as his personal mission in life.

As she grabbed her hooded sweatshirt from the closet, he got the leash from the hook in the hallway and brought it to her.

"Aww, aren't you cute?" She scratched behind his ears, making his eyes close in pleasure. "Good boy. You deserve a treat."

She stuck a nasty bone-shaped cookie into his mouth. He took it carefully between his teeth, trying not to break it and keeping his tongue away from touching it.

After they'd left the apartment, Cassy stopped in the lobby to greet a neighbor and Pumpkin used the moment to spit the cookie out, dropping it into the pot with a palm tree. Dog treats smelled like shit. But Cassy always seemed so happy when feeding them to him. She made a really big deal out of it every time, and he had no heart to spit them out in front of her, trying to do it discreetly.

"Going to the park, Cass?" Mister Riley waved at them from behind the front desk. "Have fun, Pumpkin."

Pumpkin wagged one of his tails in the man's direction. He didn't mind Mister Riley, who'd always been nice to Cassy. Mister Riley was the only man in the Universe, other than Cassy's dad, whom Pumpkin trusted to be in Cassy's phone contacts.

Chapter 3

Cassy

"Get it, Pumpkin! Get the stick!" The stick I'd tossed lay just a few feet away, but my dog hadn't made the slightest movement to retrieve it. "Come on, doggy." I jumped like a freaking cheerleader, waving my arms in the air. "Go, get it!"

He had that bored expression on his face he often got when I tried to make him do the stuff that other dogs *loved* doing. Lifting his hind paw, he scratched behind his ear, clearly demonstrating that fetching sticks was way beneath him.

I heaved an exasperated breath. He gave me a questioning glance, and I half-expected him to say something. Of course, Pumpkin never spoke. He hardly ever made any sound at all. But the way he looked at me sometimes made me feel like he understood so much more than he let on.

With a big yawn, he stretched. His three tails, long and fluffy like feather boas, swayed in the air like a fan of ostrich feathers held by a burlesque dancer.

I tied my hoodie around my waist. Despite it being October, the weather was mild today. Running had made me warm, too.

We'd just made the full loop around the park, jogging together. Pumpkin might be tired. But from my experience, this dog could run for hours, keeping up with a pickup truck on a mountain road. He'd done that before when my parents and I went camping. So, I knew for a fact that a few miles of jogging in the park wouldn't kill him.

He loved running. His mouth open, his tongue dangling to the side, he'd looked like he was smiling, running his head off. He'd play fetch too on occasion. Especially when we had no time or space to run. But he clearly wasn't in the mood to play today.

"Are you going to get that stick or not?" I propped my hands on my hips.

He rolled his eyes at me. I swore he did. I know dogs weren't supposed to have many facial expressions. But this dog... I loved him to bits, but he drove me nuts with his attitude sometimes.

Turning around, he sauntered over to the stick, picked it up, and carried it back to me, as if doing me a huge favor.

"See? You can do it!" I clapped my hands before taking the stick from him. "I know you're smart."

"Smart but lazy, isn't he?" a male voice sounded behind me.

I turned around to find a smiling blond guy standing on the walking path. He was wearing a sky-blue polo shirt and a pair of jeans. And his smile was kind of cute.

"What breed is your dog?" He tipped his chin at Pumpkin.

"Oh, we still haven't established that for sure." I laughed. "He's a mix of a few. A corgi. A collie or a sheltie, maybe? A very tall one. With some birth abnormalities thrown in."

I bent to pet Pumpkin's head. His bored expression was now gone. His pointy ears stood to attention, as if listening to every word exchanged between me and the stranger. His multi-colored eyes closely watched the newcomer.

"Abnormalities?" the man asked. "Like the three tails?"

"Yeah. The vet suggested we remove two. Surgically." I winced. The thought of putting Pumpkin under a scalpel just to make him look more "conventional" made me sick to my stomach. "The tails don't seem to bother him, though. So, we let them be."

"He sure is unique." The man agreed, then offered his hand to me. "I'm Mathew, by the way."

"Cass." I shook his hand, hoping I didn't stink too much like sweat after my run.

His smile stretched wider as he held on to my hand for a moment longer than was necessary. "It's very nice to meet you, Cass."

An older man passed by on a bike along the path. Placing his hand on the small of my back, Mathew steered me out of the bike's way and onto the grass.

Pumpkin flattened his ears against his head. A deep rumble vibrated in his throat. Mathew threw him a wary glance, jerking his hand away from me.

"Oh, don't worry. He never hurt a fly in his life. He doesn't even bark. Ever." I ruffled the fur on top of my dog's head. He shot me a glare from under his brow. "Do you have a dog?" I asked Mathew.

"No. But my aunt does. Hers is a white, fluffy thing, the size of a squirrel." He laughed.

I kind of liked the sound of his laughter. It made me smile, too.

"It barks non-stop," he added.

Pumpkin seemed to relax about Mathew a little. Or more like, he appeared to be distracted by something else. He lifted his nose, sniffing the wind. Pacing in circles, he stared at the sky.

Mathew noticed his odd behavior. "What is he looking at?"

He tilted his head up. I looked up as well. There was nothing but a clear sky above us.

"Not sure," I said. "A bird, maybe? Or a squirrel in that tree?"

Pumpkin had never shown much interest in birds or squirrels before. Holding his nose up, he trotted away from us and around some trees. This was an off-leash area of the park. Still, I didn't want him to wander off too far.

"I should put the leash—" I started.

"Hands in the air!" someone shouted up the path, just behind the bushes that grew alongside it.

"Freeze!" Another voice yelled. "Or I'll shoot."

I backed away from the hedge. "What in the world..."

A man in a worn leather jacket jumped from behind the bushes. He nearly tripped over me. I swerved out of his way, but he grabbed me by my neck.

"Get away from me or I'll end her!" he yelled out to someone.

Two policemen ran out of the bushes, holding guns.

"I'll kill her, I said." A cold blade pressed against my neck, robbing me of air.

My spine snapped straight, going rigid. Holy ginger biscuits... How did I get myself into this?

Mathew was nowhere in sight. He must've run away. Smart man. I would've run, too, if I could.

What *could* I do?

Through the fog of shock and fear, I remembered the self-defense spike my dad had given me the year I started college. It was the size of a pen, with a sharp end and indentations for a better grip. I had it attached to my keychain ring but hadn't needed to use it. Until now.

With shaking fingers, I reached for my waist pack where my phone and keys were along with the small bag of Pumpkin's treats.

"Don't move." My attacker yanked me to him, shoving the blade closer.

I froze, afraid to breathe. With every breath and every swallow, I felt the cold steel of the knife at my throat more acutely.

"Let her go," a policeman ordered.

The other one quietly said into the black communication device strapped to his shoulder, "We have a hostage situation."

Hostage.

That was me. I was the hostage. Cold dread slithered down my back. Despite my best efforts to keep calm, a whimper escaped me.

"Drop your fucking guns," the guy croaked at my ear. "Or I'll cut her fucking throat!"

"Just calm down, okay?" The policeman lifted his hands in a pacifying gesture.

Did that actually *pacify* my attacker? I couldn't see his face, but the press of the knife against my neck was as strong as ever. I guessed it didn't calm him down at all.

A crescendo of thuds came from behind me. It sounded like a horse running on a soft carpet. Or a very large dog dashing across the grass lawn.

My attacker jerked suddenly. Air was knocked out of his chest with a strangled sound. He dropped the knife, and I spun out of his grip.

Next, my monster of a dog leaped on top of the guy.

"Pumpkin!" I yelled, afraid to believe I was free again.

My dog looked bigger than ever. His claws extended. He dug them into the dirt, pinning the man's wrists down with his front paws. His tails coiled around the guy's legs, keeping him spread like a starfish on the ground.

The thick fur on the back of Pumpkin's neck stood up, making it look like a lion's mane. His jaw grew and expanded, opening wide, like that of a boa constrictor. It allowed Pumpkin to fit the entire head of the wretched criminal into his mouth. Only the man's matted dark hair was sticking out between the long, knife-like teeth of my pet. The blue-and-green eyes of the dog I knew since he was a puppy, were suddenly bright red. So bright, they appeared to glow.

"What the fuck is this?" Both policemen raised their guns, now pointing them at Pumpkin.

"No! Please, don't shoot." I waved my hands, jumping between my dog and their guns.

A policeman frowned.

"Stand back, ma'am," he warned.

"Just... Let me get my dog," I pleaded. "He's not going to hurt anyone."

The criminal on the ground jerked his legs. What if Pumpkin suffocated him with his mouth? If there was a single scratch on this thug, we could get in so much trouble. They'd take Pumpkin away. They might even order us to put him to sleep...

My hands shook as I tried to reach for him.

"Pumpkin, no! Leave it." I prayed that for once he'd listen to a command on the first try. "Come here, boy!"

Obedience never was an automatic thing with my dog. No matter how hard I trained him, he always seemed to pick and choose which commands to follow and when.

My heart beat so hard, I felt it in my throat.

"Come on, Pumpkin. Come to me now."

He rolled his shoulders side to side. The fur on the back of his neck finally flattened, lying down.

"That's a good boy." I took out a dog treat from the pouch around my waist. "Come, Pumpkin. Look what I've got for you."

He stepped off the man, and the policemen quickly moved in. One of them snapped the handcuffs on. The other one promptly read the guy his rights.

Onlookers had gathered around us, coming closer now that there was no more immediate danger for anyone.

"That dog isn't right," someone said.

"It looks weird," another one agreed.

Pumpkin's eyes no longer glowed red, and his jaw shifted back into its regular size and shape. But the memory of the terrifying image of him holding the man's head in his mouth would forever stay with me.

I wrapped an arm around my dog. "He was just protecting me."

The two policemen hauled the criminal up to his feet. His hair dripped with the dog's saliva. He cringed, trying to wipe it off his face with his shoulder. Thankfully, I didn't spot any bites or even a scratch on him anywhere.

"This animal is huge," someone said, "and looks dangerous."

"He didn't hurt anyone," I insisted.

A woman scrunched her nose, giving Pumpkin a once-over. "He may be rabid. Just look at those teeth."

I grabbed Pumpkin's jaw with both hands and forced his mouth closed. "He's healthy and generally well-behaved. He's up to date on all his vaccinations, including the rabies shots."

"Yeah? He looked like he was about to bite that guy's head off."

"He didn't *bite* anyone." My voice sounded high with panic.

The policemen were too occupied with their newly arrested criminal to pay us any attention. I wondered if they'd want me to give a statement or something. On the other hand, they saw everything that happened with their own eyes. There was nothing I could add to their case. They obviously knew this guy better than I did.

"Come, Pumpkin." I clipped the leash on to his collar, eager to lead him away from the hecklers.

His body vibrated under my hands. He seemed wired, barely containing his aggression. For the first time ever, I feared I might not be able to control him if he turned violent again. I'd never seen him like that before. What he'd just done with his jaw and eyes... What the hell had that been?

Maybe these people were right? Was he dangerous?

But I'd known my dog for over a decade. He might be big, but he was harmless. He'd never hurt anyone. Even now, he'd knocked the thug to the ground, but he hadn't harmed him in any way other than slobbering all over him.

I raked my fingers through the thick fur around Pumpkin's neck. "It's all good, buddy. Let's go get some ice cream. Okay? We earned it today."

I gently led him off the path and onto the grass behind some trees, away from the suspicious crowd. Thankfully, he followed without so much as a pull on the leash. Once we were out of sight, I stepped behind the trunk of a tree and plopped down on the ground.

"I just need a moment."

I had to catch my breath, to rub away the phantom sensation of the cold blade pressed to my neck. To gather my thoughts.

Pumpkin looked like he could use a minute, too. Lying on the ground, he scooted closer, then put his head in my lap.

"Are you okay?" I petted his big head.

A tendril of apprehension still lingered somewhere deep inside me. It'd been so new to see Pumpkin display aggression. He'd been lazy, dismissive, and stubborn at times. He would ignore people and commands he didn't like. On a few occasions, he'd growled. But he'd never attacked anyone before. Not until today.

I dipped my head to see his eyes. They were their usual color now—one blue, one green. I stroked his head again. It was my Pumpkin. The pet I'd had for a decade now. He'd seen me laugh and cry. We'd watched TV together, went for walks daily, and slept in the same bed for the past ten years.

"Thanks for looking after me." I hugged him and placed a kiss on his furry forehead. "Now, how about that ice cream?"

He jerked his tails in a wagging attempt, then lifted his nose up again.

"What is it, buddy?"

He leaped up to his paws.

"Pumpkin?" I got up, too, unnerved by his unusual behavior.

Just like before, he started pacing in circles as if about to take someone's scent. Except that instead of sniffing the ground, he kept holding his nose up, drawing air in through his nostrils.

Suddenly, he took off.

"Pumpkin!" I yelled, sprinting after him. "Stop! Come back!"

I ducked to grab the leash dragging behind him and missed. He ran faster, getting out of my reach. This dog could outrun a truck. Fat chance I'd ever catch up with him if he really meant to get away. But why would my dog want to run away from me?

"Pumpkin!"

He stopped abruptly in the middle of a clearing between the trees. And I saw what he'd been staring at.

A silver disk descended from above and hovered over my dog. The surface of the disk was so highly polished, it reflected the sky around it, making the disk almost invisible in the shimmering sunlight.

What on earth was it? A flying saucer?

For real?

A cone of green light descended from the middle of the disk all the way down to Pumpkin. Then my dog was lifted off the grass, moving up the light beam.

The freaking aliens were abducting my dog!

Panic jolted me to run even faster.

"Oh no, you're not!" I dashed toward the disk, determined not to let them get away with it. "Pumpkin!"

He kicked his paws inside the light beam, but it got him nowhere. The column of light kept steadily sucking him upwards. He kicked faster, looking desperate, then turned his head to me and...barked. For the first time ever, I heard my dog bark. It was a sharp, deep sound, like no bark I'd heard before. But he was clearly calling to me for help.

"I'm coming, buddy." I ran as fast as I could, my heart beating high in my throat, my legs burning.

I jumped into the light and grabbed onto his hind paws.

"Got you!"

My feet lifted off the ground. My hoodie loosened from around my waist and fell.

Pumpkin wrapped his tails around my wrists, holding on tight, as both of us ascended higher and higher up the beam of alien light.

Chapter 4

Cassy

It was freezing cold. I shivered and pulled my legs up to my chest. Where was my blanket? And more importantly, where was Pumpkin? He'd keep me warm better than any blankets.

I patted the space around me in search of him. Instead of bedding, my hand touched hard rubber and cold metal.

Where was I? I jolted awake with a start.

It was a large and barren place. Dark. Only a strip of reddish light under the ceiling illuminated the room. The walls and floor were made of black metal in fluid lines with rounded corners. Textured rubbery runners covered the floor.

I had no idea what this place was supposed to be. I'd never been here before. I'd never even seen anything like this in real life. Was this a dream?

"Hello?" I sat up.

I was still wearing my exercise clothes—long leggings and a sports bra—which certainly didn't provide enough layers for how cold it was in here. I rubbed my arms, hugging myself.

"Is anyone here?" I called again.

There was no answer.

With cold fingers, I fumbled with the zipper of my waist pack. My phone was still there, along with my keys and the few remaining dog treats. Releasing a breath of relief, I yanked the phone out.

My relief was short-lived. The phone was dead. Its black lifeless screen greeted me with no response to my frantic pushing at it or the buttons.

Well, that was no help. I put the useless device back into my waist pack. At least, I seemed to be unharmed. Nothing hurt when I pushed up to my feet. Nothing was broken.

I tried to focus, forcing my thoughts back to the last moments I remembered.

The park. The thug in an old leather jacket. His cold blade pressed to my neck...

I rubbed my throat. The soreness was still there. The incident in the park hadn't been a dream. Which meant the flying saucer must have been real, too.

Did aliens really take my dog? The notion was ridiculously insane. But what other explanation did I have?

"Pumpkin? Where are you, boy?"

I'd had him, hadn't I? I'd grabbed his paws. Somehow, we still got separated. I seemed to be the only one here.

Where was *here?*

Where the hell was I?

I turned around slowly, surveying the place. Dark metal and rounded walls surrounded me. But there was an arched opening in the far wall. It looked like a door. Hugging my arms, I staggered in that direction.

The opening led me to a long corridor, just as poorly lit as the large room before it. The red lighting strip above cast an eerie red glow onto the dark metal walls, making the space look like something out of a nightmare.

Maybe I really was sleeping? I was dreaming all of this. And when I'd wake up, Pumpkin would be right there, in bed with me, safe and sound.

If this was a dream, I wished to get out of here as soon as possible. I pinched my arm. It felt disturbingly realistic, and the nightmare didn't stop.

"Pumpkin!" I called again, just in case.

And just like before, I got no answer.

I padded along the corridor. There were more arched doors on each side along the walls. I knocked on a few with no answer. They all appeared to be locked. No matter how hard I pulled or shoved, they wouldn't budge.

What was this place? It smelled like nothing. The air had that sterile, processed quality to it. It was breathable, but without any scent at all.

"Hey!" I slammed my fist into yet another locked door. "Is there anyone here?"

The echo of my fist hitting against the metal reverberated through the empty corridors. Empty. I was the only one here. The chilling realization made me shudder.

After wandering through the corridors that seemed endless, I came upon another arched entrance in the wall. This one was wide open, leading me into a large, round room.

The circular floor was surrounded with rows of seating, each row positioned higher than the one before, like in a theater or a circus. However, the minimalistic look of black-and-white metal here would fit better with some utilitarian purpose rather than one of entertainment.

If this was a theater, it looked more like a medical theater than one for performing arts. I could easily imagine an operating table set in the middle of the floor, a group of mad scientists performing some out-of-this-world surgery for others to watch.

Or maybe mad scientists would present the results of their experiments to other crazy geniuses who made things like spooky Frankenstein's monsters, patched together from human and animal parts.

Dread shook me. This room seemed even colder than the rest. I rubbed my upper arms, ready to leave this place, when a door on the opposite end of the floor caught my eye. I might as well make sure that one was locked, too, before leaving.

I crossed the floor, my fist raised, ready to knock. A growl came from behind the rows of seats on both sides of me.

"Hello?" I asked hesitantly.

A giant black dog leaped from behind the first row of seats. With its teeth bared, saliva dripped from its fangs. It growled in warning, its ears pressed to its head.

Struck by shock and fear, I staggered away from it.

Another dog leaped out from the opposite direction. This one looked even more vicious than the first one. Its barks sounded like gunshots, sharp and deafening.

I shrank away from them, fear lodged in my throat, making it hard to breathe. The beast snapped its sharp teeth at me. I tripped, scurried on all fours, then jumped to my feet and ran.

Blinded by terror, I paid little attention to where I was running, just trying to get away from the monsters chasing me. Their barks and growls sounded close behind me. Way too close.

Fear spurred me on, giving me speed. I dashed through the corridors. The walls and the doors merged into a blur. Running around a corner, I brushed my hand along a door. Blue and green lights lit up when my fingers touched a small panel on the side.

I skidded to a stop.

The dogs seemed to have fallen back. I heard no more barking or growling. Placing my hands on my knees, I gasped for air, catching my breath. The lights on the door panel went off. I slammed my hand against it, turning them back on.

Shapes and characters I'd never seen before flashed in green and blue on the screen. I poked at them randomly. Nothing happened. If this was a combination lock, it could take me ages to figure out the right sequence. It could also be programmed to someone's palm or fingerprint. Then I'd be just wasting my time, endlessly poking at the flashing screen.

A thunderous roar suddenly came from deep inside the facility. It rolled through the walls and corridors like a swell of horror, much deeper and louder than those of the dogs before.

A new wave of terror shook me. My knees grew weak. I leaned with my back against the door, struggling to stay upright.

The roar grew into a blood-curdling howl.

A shudder ran through me. A spike of adrenaline urged me to run again. But how far could I run in this maze of corridors? I hadn't eaten or drunk anything since I'd woken up on that rubber floor. If I kept running aimlessly, I'd collapse soon from thirst and exhaustion.

Instead, I had to find a place to hide.

I unzipped my waist pack. The only thing it had besides the useless phone and dog treats was my house key. The key to our apartment was small, but the self-defense spike on the keychain could be handy. I took it out and wrapped my fingers around its knobby length. Using all the strength I had, I stabbed the lit-up panel with the sharp end. The glass cracked, and I stabbed harder, breaking it more.

After scooping the broken glass out of the panel. I pulled out a whole bunch of flat see-through pieces connected by white, hair-thin filaments that filled the cavity behind the screen. These must be the electronic components used to operate the screen and hopefully the lock in the door. But I had no time to examine them in any detail.

A dead silence hovered in the corridor now, even more menacing than the growls and howls had been. Worry prickled my skin, urging me to hurry. There was no way to predict when the next sound would come, where it would come from, or what it'd be. A growl? A roar? Or snapping of teeth just above my ear?

Shaking in fear, I stuck my fingers inside the cavity of the broken panel to find the stubby end of the deadbolt. All those fancy lights and plastic parts were there to move this one part in and out of the door to lock or unlock it. I managed to grip the short end with my fingernails and pulled. The thick, polished bar slid out, and the door opened.

An alarm blared, making me jump. The silence was shattered by its wailing noise.

I had to get out of this corridor, the sooner the better. I poked my head inside the room I'd just broken into. It looked like a cabin with bunk beds, a sink, and what appeared to be a small bathroom behind a partially open wall panel. It seemed empty, so I slipped inside it and slid the door closed behind me.

After I'd shoved the deadbolt back into place, the alarm stopped. I crouched by the hole in the door left in place of the panel.

A part of me hoped to hear footsteps of people rushing to investigate what had set off the alarm. The eerie emptiness of this place weighed heavily on me. I longed to see people, even if they ran in here to arrest me. But all was quiet once again.

Why have the alarm in the first place when there was no one to hear it?

I stepped away from the door and glanced around my new hiding place. My thirst sent me to the sink first. When I turned on the faucet, water ran from it. It was clear as glass, making me feel even more thirsty. I searched for a cup or a mug, but if any of the wall panels around the sink hid cabinets behind them, I didn't find a way to open them.

The only dish I found was an empty bowl that stood under a nozzle of a device that vaguely resembled a soft-serve ice-cream machine. When I touched the device, a screen lit up. But it had unfamiliar signs and characters, and I couldn't figure out what the machine was for or how to get it to work. Instead, I used the bowl to pour some water into it.

In the dim, red light of the room, I inspected the water. It smelled like nothing at all. I dipped a finger into it—again nothing unusual happened, it just made my finger wet like water was supposed to do. I licked a drop off my finger. It had no taste of any chemicals or anything else.

I was so thirsty, my tongue felt bigger than my mouth. My throat was so dry it hurt to breathe.

Fuck it. I figured if I were to die in this place, I'd rather die from the poisoned water, hopefully quickly, rather than from a torturous, slow death from thirst.

I drank, emptying the bowl in a few large gulps. Then I placed a hand on my stomach, waiting for any unusual reaction. Nothing out of the ordinary happened. I just no longer felt so damn thirsty anymore.

Completely exhausted, I climbed into the lower bunk of the bed. It was twice as wide as the top one and had a folded blanket on it. I wrapped the blanket around myself and pulled my knees up into my chest.

I still had no idea where I was, or how I got here, or even how I managed to fall asleep after everything that had happened to me that day. But I slept.

Chapter 5

Cassy

The man smiled at me. He had the most amazing smile, with dimples in both corners of his mouth. It was both adorable and panty-melting sexy. His multi-colored eyes crinkled in the corners, which made him look kind and approachable. That must be what they called "a disarming smile." It made it impossible not to trust or not to like him.

I'd seen this man before. I had a feeling I knew him well. But we'd never spoken.

He leaned in, and my heart skipped a beat. I knew he wanted to kiss me. Anticipation buzzed along my skin. My breathing halted. Heat rushed down my body, pooling low in my belly.

My vision narrowed to that irresistibly attractive smile. To his lips that I couldn't wait to feel on mine...

The kiss never happened.

I woke up with a start.

The man had been a dream. The dream I'd already had once before, a few days ago. Just like now, it'd left me so hot and bothered that I had to kick Pumpkin out of my bedroom, then I touched myself until I came hard on my hand as the dream man watched me in my mind.

The tingling pressure between my legs demanded I do the same now. I moved my hand down under the blanket. Instead of my pajama shorts, my fingers touched the waistband of my yoga leggings. I was still wearing my exercise clothes. Because I'd never made it home after the run in the park. I wasn't in my bed.

I'd been abducted.

The chilling reality rushed in like a tide of icy water. Fully awake, I sat up on the lower part of the bunk bed, in the unknown room of the unknown facility where I seemed to be the only person in existence.

I felt hungry and cold. Pumpkin was nowhere around. And this nightmare wouldn't stop. Wrapping the thin blanket around me, I fell back onto the rubbery mattress of the bunk bed and cried.

There was no way of telling how long my meltdown lasted. But after crying for a while, the self-pity eased. I could think again. I wiped the tears away and got out of the bed.

I used the tiny bathroom that was the size of a small shower stall. The holes in the ceiling, I assumed, would be where the water came out. There was a square drain in the floor and an oddly shaped toilet by the wall. The waste disappeared the moment I'd finished. A spray of fragrant water from below made me squeak. It was followed by a warm blast of air to dry my nether regions.

Well, I might die here from fear and hunger, but at least my ass would be sparkling clean and smelling like flowers. The thought made me smirk. I shook my head, leaving the bathroom.

Next, I washed my hands in the sink, then drank some water to quench my thirst and fool the hunger. Afterwards, I searched the room for something I could use as a weapon. My self-defense spike was great, but it was too short. I needed something longer that I could use in case of an attack by a rabid hound or two.

Someone had to feed those dogs, to look after them, to train them to keep intruders like myself away. If there were any people in this place, I figured, they would likely be behind that door in the "medical theater"—the one that the dogs guarded so viciously.

The top bunk had a shiny metal bar attached to the edge of it, to prevent people from falling off, I imagined. I climbed on the bottom bunk and tried to wiggle the bar free. It looked solid. When I shoved harder, the top bunk snapped closed against the wall. It was designed to be put away when not in use. The safety bar clanked against the metal wall. To put the bunk away properly, the safety bar had to be folded in.

I pulled the bunk open again. Without folding the bar in, I slammed the bunk closed again. The bar hit the wall with a slamming noise. I repeated the steps, wrecking a perfectly good bunk bed. After a few loud slams, the bar wobbled. I grabbed it, yanking hard against the hinges. Putting all my weight on it, I hung off the loose bar, and it broke.

I fell, rolled off the bottom bunk, and hit my hip, landing on the floor. But I also had a shiny new weapon in my hands now. It was long enough to shove into a hell hound's mouth before it would get close enough to bite me.

Armed with the bar, I slid the deadbolt open and shoved at the door. The alarm blared again. I winced, pulling my head into my shoulders. On one hand, I'd just announced to the entire world that I was awake and out of my hiding place. On the other hand, there seemed to be no one to care about that, anyway.

I left the door open and the alarm blaring. If it didn't turn off automatically at some point, it would help me find my way back here later. Wandering through these identical corridors could be disorienting.

I turned left and headed down the corridor. I couldn't exactly remember where the medical theater was. Yesterday, I blindly ran in panic, trying to get away from the vicious dogs. Now, I just moved following my instincts and whatever sense of direction I possessed.

I had a feeling I went in circles for a while. Some sections of the corridors started to look suspiciously familiar. But they all also looked so alike. The sound of the alarm seemed to move closer, then farther away. I tried to get away from it, taking turn after turn.

Finally, I found the arched doorway into the spooky round room. Holding my weapon in front of me, I entered cautiously.

There were no growling noises. Keeping an eye on the seats nearby, I approached the door on the opposite end of the round floor.

"Hello?" I raised my fist, ready to pound on the door.

A loud hiss made me pause. I gripped my metal bar tighter. But instead of a dog, a snake slithered from under the door. It grew bigger right in front of my eyes. A hood opened wide on its head. Long fangs extended, glistening with venom.

Fear gripped my heart with icy fingers. Holding the bar in front of me, I took a slow step back.

Was it a cobra? By the look of its hood, it must be. But did cobras grow this big? The snake's body was as thick as my waist, and it kept expanding.

How did it even fit under the door in the first place? There was no gap between it and the floor.

Stumbling away from it, I tripped and fell backwards. The snake launched forward. I jerked my hands up, jamming the bar between the snake's jaws.

And...the bar went right through its head. The snake was sliced in two. The two halves then quickly merged into the hissing giant snake again.

"What the hell?" I sat on the floor.

The snake hissed and swayed my way again. I poked at it with my metal rod. It easily went through the snake's body that suddenly thinned, wavering like a patch of green fog in front of me. The next moment, the snake was gone, disappearing into the air.

"What was that?" I jumped to my feet, finding myself completely alone again. That didn't calm me down at all. On the contrary, the ghost-snake's bizarre disappearance left my hands clammy and my insides buzzing with unease.

"What is this place?" I whispered, afraid to make a loud noise in the eerie silence that reigned in this weird, dimly lit room once again.

I felt like running. But where? I would run faster and farther than was humanly possible if only it brought me *somewhere* out of here. Sadly, it'd probably just make me tired and get me lost. Drawing in a few deep breaths, I remained in the round theater room.

Gripping my "weapon," I approached the door that the ghost-snake had defended. Whatever was kept behind it must be worth all that effort. Which meant I had to see it, even if more ghosts showed up and threatened to suck my soul out of my body or whatever ghosts did to people.

Thankfully, no ghouls appeared when I ran my fingers over the door and found the side panel. It lit up under my touch. Using the bar, I smashed the panel, then pulled out all its see-through plastic guts. Finding the deadbolt, I hooked it with my fingernails and pulled.

Alarms blared, louder than before. I dropped my bar and slammed my hands over my ears as the door slowly opened. The room inside was pitch-black. Not even the red glow illuminated it.

Two red dots appeared inside in the darkness. Was this some kind of lighting? The dots disappeared, then appeared again, growing bigger.

Not a sound could be heard over the deafening alarm. Then a deep rumble rolled through the room. I didn't *hear* it with my ears. I *felt* it. The floor vibrated under my feet. The air shifted. The rumble resonated through my chest, making me cough. The sound grew into a roar, louder than the alarm.

The two dots moved closer, turning into a pair of red, glowing eyes. A giant mass jumped my way from the back of the room.

I spun on my heel and ran.

This was bigger than any animal I'd ever seen, faster than anything of its size. Its footfalls thundered on the metal floors behind me, shaking the entire place, as I dashed across the arena of the theater.

I'd dropped my metal bar and now had no weapon. There was no place to hide. My only hope was to make it to the room where I'd spent the night, and lock the door before this thing had caught up with me. Then I could only pray that the monster didn't have the intelligence to figure out how to unlock the door to my hiding place and that it lacked the strength to break through it.

Another roar shook the walls around me. It sounded right behind me. Too close for me to make it back to my room. Still, I pushed my legs to run faster.

A heavy paw slammed into my back, sending me flying down the corridor. I landed face down, and a heavy weight plopped on top of me.

The weight shifted and a clawed paw flipped me over, as if I were a mouse, caught by the cat that wished to play. I brought my arms up to push the monster away. My hands sank into the thick, long fur that felt...familiar.

"Pumpkin?" I opened my eyes, staring straight into the face of my dog. Except that it was twice as big as it used to be.

His eyes glowed red. His teeth were as long as my fingers. And his jaw was open wide, as if ready to swallow me whole.

"Pumpkin," I pleaded in a weak, shaky voice. "It's me, buddy. Cass. Remember? Do you... Do you want a treat?" With a trembling hand, I reached for my waist pack.

He scowled, then closed his mouth but kept his teeth bared, his lips pulled back.

"Pumpkin," I called to him sweetly.

Stretching his neck to me, he sniffed the air, then pressed his cold wet nose to my collarbone. Fear eased its grip on me, and I was able to draw in a breath.

"That's right. It's me, boy. I found you after all, didn't I?" I raked my fingers through the thick, white fur on his neck.

I did find him. But what had happened to him? This wasn't the Pumpkin I knew. He was a few times bigger than his previous size. His head looked massive, and so did his jaw and his shoulders. The three tails lashed around like whips. His claws pierced through the rubber floor mats, scraping against the bare metal underneath.

This was a monster straight from a nightmare. With Pumpkin's fur but, sadly, not much else. He looked unrecognizable.

"No worries, buddy." At this point, I kept talking mostly for my own sake. The sound of my voice was the only thing that kept me sane. "We'll figure out how to get back home. Then, I'll take you to the vet, and she…" I honestly had no idea what the vet could do for him. She seemed confused enough by what Pumpkin used to look like before. I hardly doubted she would know what to do with him now.

His jaw made a weird clicking sound. His bones appeared to slide back into place, making his face far more recognizable now and his body smaller. The fur lay down. He blinked, and his eyes weren't red anymore. One turned blue, the other one green. I released a long breath. He seemed back to normal again.

I had no idea what had just happened, but I couldn't dwell on it. Seeing my dog again as his normal self helped me relax. And with it, the strength seemed to seep out of my muscles.

"Help me up, Pumpkin, would you?" I wrapped my arms around his neck, then pulled myself up to my feet.

All this running in fear cost calories. I'd been burning through them like crazy with nothing to replenish my energy. I hadn't eaten anything since breakfast that morning before going to the park.

I shuffled down the corridor, toward the room with the bunk beds. "I need to lie down now. Take a nap. Then, I'll think about how to get us out of here. Okay?"

My empty stomach twitched with pangs of hunger. Maybe sleeping for a little while would let me forget about food for a bit? Maybe it'd give me some energy, too?

The alarm from the medical theater still sounded behind me. But I could no longer hear the one from my cabin. It must've shut down on its own. When I finally came upon the open door to my room, it was all quiet here.

"Come on." I gestured for Pumpkin to enter. "We'll get some rest."

I fed him a dog treat. While he ate it, I took a long drink of water, then gave him some too. My stomach rumbled. I wondered how long it would be before I'd decide to split the last dog treat with Pumpkin. Maybe I should do it already? It wasn't like any other food was coming my way anytime soon. I was so hungry, eating a dog biscuit didn't sound that repulsive at this point.

"It's cold." I climbed on the bed and under the blanket. "Come here." I opened the blanket, allowing Pumpkin to climb under it with me.

When I wrapped my arms around him, it almost felt like I was back home again. Pressed to his big, furry body, I finally stopped shaking. Then the echo of the nightmare made me shift away from him.

"Pumpkin?"

I took his face in my hands, studying it carefully. Every feature was familiar. I'd painted and drawn this face for many school projects and in every family portrait. He had looked bored or cheeky, sweet or goofy, but this dog's face had been a part of all my happy childhood memories. This was my Pumpkin.

"Just, you know... Don't turn into that red-eyed monster while I sleep, okay? Don't accidentally bite my head off or something."

He snorted, shifting closer, then buried his nose in my neck.

"Just a little nap, okay?" I pressed my cheek to his furry forehead. "Then, we'll figure out how to get out of here."

Chapter 6

Cassy

He smiled at me, and my heart soared. How could a man's smile make me so happy? I could stare at him forever, grinning right back at him. He was like a ray of sunshine with his tousled, bright red hair.

Adoration shone in his eyes. One of them was cool blue, the other one intense green. Very unusual. But I'd seen this combination before.

Pumpkin had eyes like that. Comparing the man whose smile made me feel hot all over to my pet dog should be disturbing. It should gross me out. It most likely would later... When I woke up.

Right now, though, the familiarity of these eyes put me at ease. It made me feel comfortable around this man.

I reached out and touched his hair. A thick curl of it hung over his forehead. It felt soft, just like fur. But his face was human—straight nose, sharp-cut jawline, high cheekbones, and very kissable lips.

He licked them, staring at my mouth. His smile slipped from his face. His eyelids dropped a little. He wrapped his arms around me, drawing me closer.

"Kiss me," I whispered, afraid he'd disappear again before anything happened. I felt I could die for one single kiss from him.

He touched the tip of my nose with his. It felt so cute and playful, I giggled. He growled softly, finally taking my mouth with his.

Oh, this was better than any kiss I'd ever had with anyone else. Though, it wasn't that technical at all.

At first, he simply pressed his mouth to mine. Warm and tender, there was comfort in the contact. I parted my lips, and he did the same, gently sliding his lips between mine.

The kiss was sweet, unhurried, like a long drink of fresh water. And I wished for it to go on forever.

He moved his hand up my back and under my sports bra. The other one traveled down under the waistband of my leggings and into my underwear. His warm, large palm cupped my backside.

I moaned into his mouth. His thigh pressed between my legs, and I rubbed myself against his hard leg muscles. The pressure between my legs tingled and grew. I pressed harder, needing more.

Oh God, it was so good.

He moved his hand under my bra from my back to my front. His hand cupped my breast, and I arched into his touch. Heat coursed through me. My nipples hardened and ached. Need pulsed between my legs.

He flexed his hand on my ass, drawing me closer. My thigh ended up between his legs, where...something stirred. It swarmed like a nest of snakes.

What the...

He kissed my neck.

"Cassy," he groaned, sounding drunk or delirious or both.

Kneading my breast, he slid my bra up. He pinched my nipple, and my eyes flew open.

This wasn't a dream!

A man was holding me, his hands in my pants and...other places. His thigh was wedged between my legs. My hips gyrating, I was rubbing myself against him shamelessly.

I shoved my hands against his chest.

"Off!"

He clearly didn't expect that. Tipping back, he lost his balance and rolled off the bed onto the floor.

"Who the fuck are you?" I yelled, searching for the self-defense spike in my waist pack.

Lying on his back, he propped himself up on his elbows and blinked at me, looking as if the answer to that question was as puzzling to him as it was to me.

Focus returned to his expression as he slid his gaze down my body. I followed it to my bra. It was still hiked up. My left boob, the one he'd caressed and pinched, was hanging out. He swallowed, licking his lips as if salivating at the thought of licking and devouring my body.

"Dammit." I yanked the bra back in place, then stuck my spike out at him. "I asked, who are you?"

"Why do I keep dreaming about you?" rushed through my brain. But I didn't ask *that* question out loud. It would've sounded too much like a confession I wasn't ready to make.

I looked around, searching for Pumpkin. He wasn't in the room. The door appeared locked, but Pumpkin was gone. This guy was the only one with me here.

"Where is my dog?" I demanded. "What did you do to him?"

He pressed his lips together and sat up. Bending one knee, he rested an elbow on it and tilted his head to one side.

"Cassy, I hate to break it to you..." he said in a deep, rumbling voice that caressed something deep inside me, making my toes curl, "but you've never actually had a dog."

I opened my mouth, ready to argue, and...shut it. There had always, *always* been a doubt in my head about *what* Pumpkin actually was. The confusion wasn't just about the breed. I'd told people he was a dog. I wished to think that was true. But if someone had offered me any other explanation to his human-like moods and attitude, to his higher-than-normal intelligence, to his acute perception that I often read in his eyes, I would've loved to hear it.

Also, how did this man know my name?

I stared at him with suspicion. "*What* did I have?"

He spread his hands aside. His dark-brown eyebrows rose in an open expression.

"Me, Cassy. You've had me."

I dropped my hand with the spike into my lap.

"What are you?"

The dim lighting of the room was enough to see his red tousled hair or fur, just like that of the man in my dreams. But there was more.

His ears were pointy, covered in velvety red fur. They stuck straight up. He wasn't wearing any clothes. His arms, legs and shoulders remained bare, but thick, white fur wrapped around his neck like a collar of a luxurious coat. It stretched down his chest, between the hard squares of his abs, then tapered to a thin trail below his waist. There was no belly button, not even a dimple where one should've been.

The fur changed from white to orange below his waist. It covered his crotch area completely. Some of it grew on his inner thighs, but most of his legs remained furless. Both his feet and hands were coal-black, the color of Pumpkin's paws. The black merged into the tan color gradually, which broke the illusion of him wearing socks or gloves—both black and tan were the colors of his skin.

"It's me, Cassy."

Shifting aside, he unfurled three long tails. Covered in long, red fur that changed to white on the tips, they swayed in the air like the most indisputable proof.

"See?"

"Wow... Well..." I scratched my head. "But how?"

"*That* I'm not sure about myself," he admitted, draping his tails over his lap. "I've been trying to figure out what I am since the day I hatched from my shell."

"You *hatched?*" This should've sounded crazy, but it actually made some sense. "You came from the pumpkin after all, didn't you?"

He nodded.

"I knew it!" I threw my hands into the air. "I knew that's what happened. You didn't sneak into the apartment like Mom tried to convince me. You came from the pumpkin. But why? And how?"

"I changed forms. I've upgraded twice now. No..." He stretched his arm in front of him, staring at it as if seeing it for the first time. And maybe this was the very first time he really took a good look at his new body. "No. I've changed three times. This is the fourth form already."

He slid his hand down his arm, then touched his chest. Following the strip of fur down his middle, he moved his hand to the patch of orange fur between his thighs. His fingers sank into it.

I cleared my throat, and he jerked his hand away from his crotch.

"Well, this is interesting," he muttered under his breath.

"Are these real?" I pointed at his ears, just to shift the focus away from whatever it was that he found so *interesting* in the fur between his legs.

"These?" He moved his ears, and it had to be the cutest thing I'd ever seen. "These haven't changed much, have they?"

"No." I smiled. "They are just as adorable as ever."

"You think I'm adorable? Even in this form?" That grin of his made an appearance, with the dimples just above the upturned corners of his mouth that gave him a cheeky look.

I blinked rapidly, turning away. "Can you just...*not* smile, please?"

"You don't like it?"

"No...It's not that. It's just a bit too much for me, right now. You know?"

"No," he sounded confused. "I *don't* know. But okay. I'll do my best not to smile."

His expression dimmed, and I immediately missed that cheeky grin of his.

"There are just so many things that are...well, crazy right now," I tried to explain, without mentioning how much that smile made me want to kiss him. "So many questions. Like what are you? Why are we here? Where are we? What happened back at the park? What is still happening?"

My voice grew higher and higher with each question. I stopped myself, afraid I'd sound hysterical if I kept talking. I took a few quick shallow breaths, closing my eyes.

He jumped to his feet. "Listen, let me feed you first. You get lightheaded and even clumsy when you're hungry. Much more emotional too. I've read it's because your blood sugar drops."

My eyes flew wide open. I should be wondering when and how he "read." But my attention focused on his promise of food.

"You'll feed me? How? There is nothing to eat. No way out of this place, either. We're stuck here—"

Hysterics threatened to explode out of me after all, but he stopped me with a kiss on my forehead. "Just give me a second."

He strolled to the soft-serve ice cream machine look-alike, somehow opened a compartment on the right of it, then took a plate out and pressed his hand to the front of the machine. The front panel lit up like a screen, with signs and characters scrolling through. He didn't press any of them, though, just continued to hold his palm flat against it.

"What is that?" I asked.

"A food replicator." He put the plate under the nozzle that dispensed some orange mash, a long sausage-like thing, and some multicolored patties. "It uses powdered nutrients to replicate the tastes and textures. Not the most appetizing thing, but it'll fill you up and give you some energy."

By now, I'd eat anything that would fill me up, even dog biscuits.

He produced a second plate, then filled it in the same fashion. From another compartment on the side, he got two utensils, then came to the bed.

"Can you hold these, please?" He handed both plates to me. "I'll also need you to get off the bed."

I did as he asked, getting up and taking the plates from him. He folded the bed into the wall, then unfolded a table and two chairs with armrests from the wall next to it.

"Let's eat." He gestured at the table.

I didn't wait for another invitation. Placing the plates on the table, I plopped into one of the chairs.

"How did you know about this?" I poked the utensil at the orange mash.

It looked very much like yams or maybe squash. The sausage seemed like it was made from finely ground meat. And the disks tasted like carrots or green peas or like some vegetables, anyway.

I'd been starving for so long, I didn't really care what exactly it was. I shoved a piece of "sausage" into my mouth. The meaty taste was pleasant enough. I followed it with a bunch of the mash and the veggie disks.

And to think that all this food was right here in the room with me all this time. I just had no clue how to access it.

"How did you know about the food replicator and how to use it?" I asked around a mouthful.

He watched me eat for a second, turning his utensil in his hand. "I believe I might be from here, Cassy."

"What do you mean?" My gaze snapped to his, even as my hand kept shoving food into my mouth.

"The systems here seem familiar."

"Familiar? Do you know where we are? What is this place? A lab? Some research facility?"

"I'm not sure what it is. Only that I belong here somehow." He leaned back with a sigh. "From the day I hatched, I've been trying to figure out who or what I am."

"Does that mean you've always been self-aware?"

"To some degree, yes."

The mash stuck in my throat. He'd always been a person. And I'd treated him like...a dog.

"I can feel electronic and communication waves," he continued. "Radio waves, too."

"How do you *feel* them?"

He tilted his head as if searching for the best way to explain. "To me, they are like wires hanging in the air. All I have to do to connect to one is just reach out with my brain and *touch* them. I can connect to any device or network, bypassing passwords or firewalls."

"Is that how you've been reading? On the Internet?"

"Yes. That's how I do my research."

"What do you research? Other than the low blood sugar in hungry humans?" I smiled.

His lips twitched, too, but he caught himself before a full-on smile had a chance to appear.

"I try to learn as much as I can. About humans, your world, your family. You."

"Me?" I blinked, my hand with the curved two-pronged fork pausing in the air.

"You have been the closest person to me all my life. My most fascinating subject to study." True to his promise, his lips didn't smile, but his eyes did. Their corners crinkled a little. The irises shone with warmth and affection.

It had a very similar effect on me as his smile did. Something fluttered in my chest, my stomach flipped, and my heart thudded faster. "What's there to study about me?"

"I learned everything I could about the books you read and the movies you watched. I researched your school, the subjects you took, and the teachers you had. I studied all I could find about your college from the moment you applied."

I stared at him, flabbergasted. "When did you do all of that?"

He shrugged. "What else did I have to do when you weren't home?"

"I thought you just napped."

He picked up a piece of sausage from his plate. "Understandable misconception, since I often lay on the couch with my eyes closed. But it helps my concentration to eliminate visual distractions."

His eloquent way of speaking prompted another question. "And...could you always talk, or is it new?"

"No. The speaking program came with the latest upgrade. I couldn't talk before. Though I did experiment with language concepts and formed complete sentences in my mind."

I'd polished the food off my plate, then dropped my chin into my hand, watching him eat. If this was his first time in this body, he held a utensil in his hand for the first time, too. I wouldn't be surprised or offended if he ate straight from the plate, like Pumpkin used to do. But he carefully speared a vegetable disk with his two-pronged fork, then neatly put it into his mouth.

"Where did you learn how to eat like that?" I asked.

"Cassy." He tilted his head again, his ears trained on me. "I know everything you do. I grew up with you. I've watched the same shows you did. I did all your school assignments with you. You read to me when we were little, remember? I learned what you learned. We studied for all your exams together."

"*I* studied. I thought *you* were just yawning and sleeping next to me."

"No. I might've had my eyes closed occasionally, but I paid attention. I'm confident I could pass all your exams now if I had to."

"*You never really had a dog.*" I still tried to wrap my mind around that.

When I'd thought I had a goofy, lazy but lovable animal in my care, I actually grew up next to a far more intelligent being. I might've had my doubts about what Pumpkin was, but I'd still treated him as a dog all his life.

When I thought about it now, I understood the reason for his stubbornness and attitude at times. What intelligent person would truly enjoy fetching a stick over and over only for it to be tossed again and again? Pumpkin loved to play, but he preferred fun, stimulating games, like hide-and-seek. He also seemed to enjoy jogging with me or chasing me in the park. All the things I liked to do too.

"Tell me something," I said, trying to reconcile my memories of Pumpkin with the man sitting across from me. "Be honest. You didn't really like any of the dog treats I fed you?"

He put the fork down, his eyes shifting aside.

"Not really," he said carefully, as if afraid to hurt my feelings.

I flinched at his confession, but not because my feelings were hurt. I felt so guilty for pushing the boring dog food on him all his life.

"How about the kibbles? Were they any better?"

He laughed softly. "Kibbles aren't that bad, actually. They taste like nothing, like cardboard. Dog treats are worse. I think they try to make them tasty by adding some flavor, but honestly, they all just taste like shit."

I gasped at hearing him swear. My guilt shot up higher. He probably got it from me—I must've sworn in his presence occasionally. Which made me a rather irresponsible dog owner, didn't it?

Dog? No. He was *not* a dog. Never had been. I had to remember that.

God, this whole thing was messing with my head...

"My favorite time of the day," he continued to reminisce, "was when you'd come home from school or, later, from college and then we would watch TV together and you would share your snacks with me. The ham-and-Swiss sandwich is by far my favorite of everything I've tried."

I liked those times, too, when I'd lean against him on the couch, watching my favorite shows or reading a book. Pumpkin was the best at cuddling.

I couldn't think of him as Pumpkin anymore, though.

"What's your name? I have to call you something, and it can't be Pumpkin, now that you're...you know." I waved a hand at him.

He hiked a shoulder. "I don't mind Pumpkin. It's been my name for so long. I'm used to it."

"No." I couldn't allow myself to think of him as my dog or my pet. Not after I'd kissed him while half-asleep. Not when I wondered whether kissing him fully awake would feel just as wonderful. "Please. You must have some other name, other than the one I gave you. Do you remember anything before you came to live with us?"

"Not much. Before I hatched, I just remember being cold or warm. There was darkness, but not much else. But when I got here, to this place, I'd been called differently."

"Here? *Who* called you differently?" I'd been so shocked by his transformation, I'd had no chance to compare our experiences after the events in the park. "Did you speak to someone here?"

"Yes."

I sat up straighter. "Are we not alone here, after all?"

He cupped the back of his neck, his hand sinking into the soft fur. "I'm not sure. I never got to see anyone. It was just a voice."

"What did it say?"

"They addressed me as M. A. X. X. 60039. 0Q."

I made a face. "Well, that's a mouthful. What is it? It doesn't sound like a name. More like some code or serial number. An awfully long one, too."

His features shifted into a pensive frown. "A serial number? Maybe that's what it is?"

"A serial number is usually given to an object. Something that's man made. Not alive. You should have a name—"

He shook his head, making me cut my sentence short.

"That's the thing, Cassy. I don't think I was born."

"No, but you hatched. Which still means you're alive. You've been growing and developing ever since."

He pushed aside our empty plates. His chest rose as if with a bracing breath.

"I've been upgrading, growing the original components, developing my software, and producing new parts as per my design and settings."

"What settings? What are you talking about? You sound like a robot right now."

"Not exactly a robot, Cassy. A cyborg. A machine created with mechanical, electronic, and biological components that are controlled by artificial intelligence."

This made no sense. With his bright smile and intelligent eyes, he'd never looked more alive. But then I thought back to his eyes burning red and the hard click in his jaw as it shrank...

He was definitely something else.

But a machine?

"There's nothing *artificial* about you," I mumbled.

He raked his hands through the fur on his head, then blew out a breath, dropping his shoulders. "It came as a shock to me, too, Cassy. But when I analyze everything I know about myself, this is the only logical explanation."

"How is it logical?" I wouldn't give up.

"Look at me." He gestured at the fur on his body, at his pointy ears, then at his three fluffy tails.

"So? You're different. Maybe you're from another planet? All aliens look different from humans. Ivodians have even more tails than you do. And Voranians have far more fur."

There were four types of aliens that humans had come into contact with lately. Besides the two I'd mentioned, there were also Ravils and Aldraians. All of them had their own unique characteristics.

I had to admit, the man sitting across the table from me didn't look like any of them. But he could be a new, yet undiscovered species, couldn't he?

He shook his head, unconvinced. "I wish I was just another life form. Someone who had parents and a family out there somewhere. All my life experiences so far have been based on that structure of society. But I believe the voice that spoke to me was right. I wasn't born. I was created. A machine, number M. A. X. X. 60039. 0Q."

I slumped in my chair, feeling deflated. Whatever he was didn't really matter. It didn't change what he had been *to me*. I wasn't even sure why I'd argued so fiercely. Maybe because I had a hard time believing that the friendly, sexy man was really a machine that was supposed to be cold and unfeeling? Maybe it was the *unfeeling* part that rubbed me the wrong way? If I felt something for him, I sure would like for him to be able to feel it for me too.

It was just too much to take in all at once.

"Can I call you Maxx? Like the first four letters in your number?" His brow furrowed, and I hurried to explain, "Pumpkin was the name of my pet. But that's not what you are. Your number is closer to your origin. It encompasses all your forms and transformations. But it's not a name. Maxx does sound like a name, though. A pretty good one, too. It comes without any outdated expectations or any 'settings.' So, you can make whatever you like out of it. It's entirely up to you who this man Maxx is going to be." I gestured at him.

He seemed to ponder my words for a moment.

"Maxx," he said, as if trying the new name out loud. "I like it. It sounds like both my past and my future."

He rested a hand on the table and I covered it with mine. The ink-black color of his skin on his hand was much darker than the warm brown of mine.

I squeezed his hand.

"It's very nice to meet you, Maxx."

Chapter 7

Cassy

"Careful," I warned. "There are ghosts in here."

Maxx pressed a hand to a door at the end of the corridor, and it slid open smoothly. Having him walk with me through this place proved extremely convenient. I didn't have to smash any more door panels.

"Ghosts?"

After we'd eaten, we decided to search this place together to figure out exactly where we were and how to get back home.

"Yes. A ghost-snake guarded the room you were locked in." I wondered if the dogs that had made me run for the hills earlier had been ghostly creatures too. I hadn't seen or heard them since. "This place is haunted."

My voice shook, and he took my hand, squeezing it gently. "Don't be afraid. I'm with you."

Oh, it felt so good to have him with me. I no longer felt scared, lonely, or even hungry. Gratitude for him flooded my chest, but I had no idea how to express in words everything I felt.

All I could say was, "Thank you."

He nodded, leading me ahead.

"Maxx?" I was glad he'd agreed to change his name. It went well with this new form and kind of gave him a brand-new identity in my mind, too, separate from that of my pet. "Do you know what the letters in your number mean?"

His handsome features hardened, and I instantly regretted my question.

"Yes," he said somberly. "These aren't letters but words in the Ivodian language. And they mean 'extermination, lethal, bio-machine...' Nothing nice, Cassy." He waved me off.

I didn't insist on a detailed translation since he clearly didn't enjoy the topic. It didn't really matter to me, anyway. The words might not be nice, but I knew for a fact there were plenty of nice things about Maxx. We grew up together, after all.

"So, you speak Ivodian now too?" I changed the topic.

"I speak quite a few languages. It came with the latest upgrade."

His expression remained somber, and I felt the need to comfort him somehow.

"These are just words." I touched his arm. "The number was given to you by someone who didn't know you at all. That's not what you are, is it?"

He said nothing.

"Do you...feel like a machine at all?" I asked after a few more paces down the corridor.

He exhaled a brief laugh. "How *would* that feel, you think?"

"I...I don't know. Cold, mechanical, stilted."

"Like the Terminator?" He smirked.

"Maybe."

His hand tightened in mine in response and his mouth pressed into a hard line.

"Listen," I hurried to explain. "I don't want to offend you. I'm just trying to understand. You don't look like a machine. In fact, you're the opposite of one. You're warm and smiling. You talk and move in a smooth, natural way. I believe you can experience emotions in the same way any living person can. So..."

"I have no explanation for any of that, Cassy. I must be made that way."

Made.

That was the biggest difference between him and me. He didn't even have a belly button. Because he wasn't *born*. He was made.

"Do you think Ivodians made you? Since it looks like your number came from them?"

"Probably."

Ivodians came to Earth only once, a few years ago. But Maxx had been here for over a decade, at least. He couldn't have come with that ship.

Another thought occurred to me. "Technically, you're only ten years old, right?"

"Not exactly. I spent far more time in my old form, in my shell."

"So, someone on Ivodi created the egg with you inside it. They dropped it on Earth for some reason. Then they returned to get you back. It was the Ivodian flying saucer back in the park, wasn't it?"

"It must've been. It looked very much like the shuttles they used during their one and only visit to Earth."

"Why did they dump us here, then? Did the voice that spoke to you say anything about that?"

"No. It didn't."

So far, I hadn't come any closer to understanding what was going on.

"What happened to you after they took us from the park? What do you remember from that day?" I asked.

He stopped and turned to face me.

"I remember being in the park with you. The preppy polo-shirt jerk approached you."

"Do you mean Mathew? He wasn't a jerk."

"Wasn't he?" He tilted his head, one of his ears twitched as if flicking away a fly. "He took off at the slightest sight of danger, leaving you unprotected."

"As he should have. He didn't know me. What did you expect him to do? To risk his life, saving a chick he just met?"

His jaw muscles flexed, and his eyes narrowed. He said nothing, but judging by his expression, that was exactly what he expected poor Mathew to do in that situation—lay his life on the line for me, nothing less.

"It was my fault, too," he exhaled. "I shouldn't have stepped away from you."

"You were distracted," I recalled.

"Right. I sensed them."

"The flying saucer?"

He nodded. "I knew something wasn't right even before I could see them. Then, the light sucked me in. With you. But when I woke up, you weren't there." His gaze focused somewhere past me, as he recalled, "I was connected to a system. Not through waves but by wires. A whole spiderweb of them, clear and thin like hair." He lifted his hand, staring at it as if expecting the wires to spring out from his skin. "The voice said they were running diagnostics to assess what had become of me. Then it said I had a disturbing number of deviations from my core programming that would have to be corrected."

"What *deviations?*" I scoffed. "There's nothing wrong with you. Never was. You're perfect just the way you are."

"Thanks." He smiled, making me feel weak in my knees.

He caught himself again, quickly wiping the grin off his face, but I touched his hand.

"It's okay. Smile all you want, Maxx. It was a stupid request from me in the first place. No one can tell you how to express what you feel."

The truth was, in addition to making me want to kiss him, his smile also made me feel all warm and fuzzy inside, allowing me to forget the fear and dread I felt in this place. I loved seeing it, even if I had to fight the desire to kiss him all over every time it lit up his face.

"I have no idea what they meant by 'deviations,'" I said. "But there is nothing I'd change in any one of your forms."

I didn't mean it as a compliment, just stated a fact. But he beamed at me, as if he'd just received the biggest praise in his life. Once again, I had to force my attention away from that smile of his. It did things to me that made it hard to think clearly.

"Where is that person now? The one who spoke to you?" I asked. "Did it sound like a man or a woman?"

He frowned in concentration. "I don't know. It was just a voice, and it sounded rather androgynous, I'd say. I'm not sure if the person was even there. They could've been speaking remotely."

"I see." I took a moment or two to ponder his words. "You said you feel like you belong here. How exactly do you *feel* it?"

He rubbed the back of his neck.

"Well, as I said, I can connect to human networks easily enough. But they always need some time for me to untangle and figure them out at first. Here, it happens automatically. It's like all my connections were designed to work with the systems in here. It costs me no effort to open doors or operate the food replicator, for example. It all just snaps into place on its own."

"So, if you are...um, connected, can you tell me what this place is?"

He blew out a breath. "No. Only the simple things like the doors, the food replicator, and some climate controls, like the temperature settings, are open for me to access. The rest is blocked."

"But you said you can connect to anything, even bypassing passwords. That the waves are like wires hanging out in the open."

"Yes. But the 'wires' aren't exposed here. They're protected. All main systems, including communication and information, are inaccessible, like the wires would be enclosed into tubes. I can 'touch' them, but I can't get inside."

Disappointment sliced through me. He must have noticed my deflated expression and stroked my arm soothingly.

"Come, Cassy. We'll find our way out of here, I promise. We'll just need to figure out where we are."

"Okay." His reassurances gave me hope when I needed it most. My own optimism was worn to threads by now.

I followed him down the corridor. He walked half-a-step ahead of me. His fur did a decent job concealing his front. But other than his tails, he had no fur at all on his back. His butt cheeks were mostly on display. Hard muscles rolled under his smooth skin, bringing the expression "buns of steel" to mind. In his case, that could be quite literal if he really was a cyborg.

The silly thought made me snort a laugh, chasing the gloom of our situation away.

Maxx glanced at me over his shoulder, one eyebrow raised in question.

"Oh, nothing." I shook my head, then blurted out, "I just thought we should find you some pants."

"What for?" He shrugged. "My fur covers more of my body than a regular guy would cover up on a beach."

"What beaches do you go to? Have you seen yourself from the back?"

He touched his ass. But he did it so fast, he ended up slapping himself. The sound was loud enough to reverberate under the ceiling. And inexplicably, it made me wish to do the same. The desire to slap this man's ass, or at least to grab it, came on strong and randomly. I fisted my hands at my side, lest I start groping him.

He rubbed the spot he'd just slapped. "Okay, if you see a pair of pants anywhere, let me know."

His eyes lingered on mine, and my face warmed under his attention. I might've grown up with Pumpkin. But as a man, Maxx remained very much a stranger. His body had been rearranged in a new way. His voice was new. The way he looked at me was different. Far more exciting.

I wasn't sure what to do about this new attraction. Clearing my throat, I tore my gaze away from his. I slid it past his shoulder and into the corridor behind him.

A figure, shrouded in white, moved away from us.

I choked on my next breath, momentarily paralyzed by shock.

The figure appeared to move slowly but covered the length of the entire corridor quickly. As it rounded the corner, turning right, the hem of its shroud brushed by the wall. A chunk of the white material dissipated into the air, shredded into fog.

"A ghost..." I croaked, grabbing Maxx's arm.

Chapter 8

Cassy

Maxx whipped his head around, but the ghostly apparition was now gone.

"What was it? What did you see, Cassy?"

I fought a shudder that shook through my entire body and licked my dry lips. "A white ghost… It went that way." I gestured to the right.

"A ghost? Not a person?" He headed down the corridor.

I clung to his arm, afraid to stay behind on my own but also terrified to follow the ghostly creature. "No. It couldn't be a person. It's made of smoke, or fog, or something…"

We turned around the corner behind which the ghost had gone. The corridor was empty here as far as the eye could see.

"It disappeared," I whispered.

A chilly sensation pricked along my spine. I shivered, leaning closer to Maxx.

"Interesting." He didn't sound scared, but the way he said that one word, slowly and with emphasis, sent another flock of cold shivers down my skin.

He wrapped an arm around my shoulders, staring at the nearest wall. No, I realized, it wasn't the wall that caught his interest but the door in it. It looked slightly different from the other doors in the corridors. This one was made from two parts with a split in the middle.

Maxx splayed his hand on one half, then moved it to the other. A strip of running lights lit up in the middle, then the doors parted, opening into a small room with shiny metal walls.

"What's this?" I poked my head inside. The room was completely empty, cylindrical, and without windows.

"An elevator." Maxx stepped inside, leading me in.

I glanced back into the corridor. There was still no sign of the ghost, which could be both good or bad. Good, because I really didn't want to see it ever again. Bad, because if I didn't see it, it could appear anywhere, anytime, much closer to me than before.

Maxx slid a finger along a strip of purple light inside. "There are eleven floors here. We are on the one numbered minus two."

"*Minus?* Like underground?"

"Possibly." He stopped his finger on the purple line. "Two floors above us is floor zero. It's right in the middle. Should we go there?"

I tried to look and sound calm, though the unsettling vision in the corridor still haunted my mind. "May as well. If there is an exit from this place, it would likely be on the ground floor, right?"

Eleven floors. This place proved to be even bigger than I'd first thought.

The elevator moved up in a smooth motion. When the doors opened, Maxx held his arm back, keeping me inside for a second, as he scanned the space outside for any signs of danger. Satisfied it was safe, he nodded.

"Let's go." He took my arm, entering into a huge open place.

After the tight maze of corridors below, the giant room with the high ceiling made me feel like I'd stepped outside. To my disappointment, there were no people here, either.

Just like the floor below, the room was illuminated in red. The strips of light high under the ceiling were curled and bent into amazing designs that hung like red, glowing chandeliers.

But the most breathtaking feature of the room were two giant screens. They took up two entire walls on the right and the left of us, floor to ceiling. On the screens, images of stars in space were displayed.

I walked over to the one on our right.

"This is so beautiful. It almost looks 3D." I touched the surface. It felt smooth and cool under my fingers.

Maxx came beside me and splayed his hand on the screen too.

"You know what's funny," I said. "They keep the lighting low, like they want to preserve energy here. Which makes sense, since there's no one around, anyway. But then they have these giant screens turned on. And it's not just a picture. It's a video. It must take a lot of power to play this footage of outer space."

The stars twinkled. To the right, a cluster of light churned with purple and red. I wondered what astronomical event that could be.

Maxx dropped his hand from the glass. He looked grim.

"It's not a screen, Cassy. It's a window."

"A window?" I echoed.

He nodded, his shapely eyebrows moving closer together. "A giant window into space. We're not in a building, but on a spaceship."

Spaceship...

I gaped at the stars beyond the glass. These were real?

When abducted by aliens, one could expect to be taken to a spaceship, but I'd never been on one before. I'd had no idea what it was like to travel by one. This spaceship was huge and appeared stable, like a building. Other than the sterile air, nothing about it made me doubt my being still on Earth. The gravity seemed the same. There had been no sensation of moving.

I pressed my forehead to the glass. The stars, the distant galaxies, the purple-red churning flame of an unknown-to-me space phenomenon... I didn't recognize any of that. There was nothing out there that resembled Earth.

Which one of the shiny dots in the distance was my home?

The more I stared into the endless ocean of stars, the smaller I felt. Lost. Ripped away from home, with no way of getting back...

My mind was spinning. Even the giant ship now felt tiny, too, racing through eternity.

"I just want to go home," I whispered. Tears welled in my eyes, making the space swim and blur in front of me.

"Cassy." Strong arms wrapped around me. His warm chest leaned into me from behind. Maxx's body enveloped me like a warm comfort blanket.

No one called me Cassy anymore, not even my parents. For everyone out there, I was Cass or Cassidy. Only Maxx kept using my childhood name. And right now, hearing it from him felt incredibly comforting.

"We'll find a way back," he said. "I promise I'll take you home."

"How?"

We hurled through space in a haunted alien spaceship with no crew. For all we knew, there was no soul alive in this place beside us. We could fly forever, with no route to follow and no destination to arrive at. This ship was simply a tiny speck among the myriads of others in the vastness of space.

The stars seemed to spin in a vortex. I felt dizzy, but I couldn't tear my eyes away from the window.

We'd die here, in the middle of nowhere, the moment the food replicator stopped working, the water stopped running, or the air filtration system malfunctioned, and no one would know what happened to us.

The air supply system seemed to be malfunctioning already. There wasn't enough oxygen. Not for me, anyway. The more I tried to drag it into my lungs, the less air there appeared to be. I gasped, my fingers flexing, scraping the glass.

"Cassy." Maxx flipped me around, away from the dreadful stars.

But now, I was faced with a similar picture of open space in the window on the opposite side of the room. I gasped for air harder, opening my mouth like a fish out of water.

Maxx gave me a slight shake.

"Cassy, look at me." He cupped my face, turning it to him. "Look at me."

My eyes met his, and I focused on the familiar sight. One eye blue, one green. The bright specks twinkled inside both irises, like stars. Only these stars were warm and comforting, not intimidating.

"I'll get you home, do you hear me? Even if this is the last thing I do," he said firmly.

"Oh, how I wish to believe you..." I whimpered, struggling to breathe through the panic attack.

"We'll have to find the cockpit, the captain's bridge, or whatever they call it on Ivodi. From there, I'll find a way to connect to the ship's navigation systems. We'll figure out exactly where we are. Then we'll make this ship take us back to Earth." He stroked my cheekbones with his thumbs. "We'll be fine."

I sniffled. "But you said you can't connect to the systems here."

"I just haven't figured out how yet. Main controls are usually on the bridge. Once we get there, it should be easier for me to connect to the navigation system. I managed to untangle the messy networks on Earth. It should be easier here, since I'm a part of this world."

I wasn't sure whether it was his words or the smooth flow of his deep voice, but it calmed me enough for my breathing to even out somewhat.

"Are you sure?"

"Positive." He sounded confident. I feared he might be faking it for my sake, but I was grateful, nevertheless. I was so incredibly grateful to have Maxx on this ghost ship with me. I just wished I had some of his confidence.

I drew in a shaky breath, forcing myself to get a grip. "Just like you connected to our Wi-Fi back home?"

"Exactly. Wi-Fi and everything else." He wiped off the few tears I hadn't realized had escaped my eyes.

"What *everything else?*" We didn't have that much technology in the apartment.

"Radio waves, satellite signals, your phone—"

"My phone?"

He fell silent, like he'd said something he hadn't intended and now didn't know what to do about it.

I gave him a stern look. "Maxx, tell me, did you hack my phone?"

"I'm not a hacker." He sounded indignant. "Someone just had to keep an eye on your contacts and their behavior. You got a lot of new *acquaintances* when you started college."

I narrowed my eyes at him, not feeling that impressed by this revelation. At the same time, I was grateful for the distraction this topic provided. My panic attack had passed, and I no longer felt like breaking through the window and leaping into the open space beyond.

"And how exactly did you do that? Keeping an eye on my contacts?"

He glanced away, speaking with great reluctance, "I...connected to your phone. To monitor your emails and text messages. For your safety."

"But that's the actual definition of hacking, what you'd just said. Just because you did it 'for my safety' instead of fishing for my banking info doesn't make it any better."

"Doesn't it?" He tilted his head, his ears perking up.

I contemplated the ethics of both examples. "Well, maybe the concern for someone's safety justifies invasion of privacy, sometimes. But still... It's not like I really was in any danger. What did you do, anyway?"

With his hand around my shoulders, he turned toward the elevator.

"I blocked the assholes. I also intercepted and deleted their messages before you had a chance to read them and likely get upset." I sensed no remorse in his voice. He only looked a bit sheepish when he admitted, "I might've also texted one or two guys back. You know, the most stubborn ones who refused to take no for an answer."

"You texted people pretending to be me?" I huffed, anger rising in me.

"Just once or twice. I swear. And those were the guys you really had to stay away from. Like one got increasingly aggressive when he didn't get replies to his messages from you right away. And the other one sent a long list of things he expected from a woman in a relationship. He wanted you to confirm you received it, read it, and agreed to all points before he'd take you on a second date."

Wow, it appeared he had averted a few disasters coming my way. But still... This had been a serious invasion of privacy on his part.

The elevator stopped on the floor number minus two, and the doors opened. I blew out a breath and stormed out, not even checking for ghosts out in the corridor first.

"Cassy..." Maxx easily caught up with me and jogged in front of me with a pleading look on his face.

I raised a finger in warning. "Don't give me those *puppy eyes*. I can't believe I've been cock-blocked by my own dog. Repeatedly."

He sulked. "Not a *dog*."

He was absolutely right about that, but I was too riled up to admit it.

"Okay, so those two might've been a complete disaster. But I've met more than two guys in the past few years, you know. Not all of them were assholes. But thanks to you, I never even got a chance to get to know any of them. You never let me get in touch with anyone."

He remained adamant. "Trust me, I've saved you from a lot of heartbreak over the years."

I dragged a hand over my face. "You made me the last twenty-one-year-old virgin in all the Universe."

"Now, you're being overly dramatic," he said flatly.

I refused to look at him. "I thought there must be something wrong with me... That I was repulsive or something. That's why no one cared to get to know me better."

His expression fell.

"Oh, Cassy..." His voice shook either from regret or compassion. He swiftly closed the distance between us and took me into his arms. "There is nothing wrong with you. Not a single damn thing. To me, you are absolutely perfect. None of those guys deserved you."

I pressed my cheek to the fur on his chest. "They didn't? But who did? Who were you keeping me for?"

He remained quiet, and I lifted my face, needing to see his eyes.

"Who?" I repeated. "Yourself?"

He gave me a humorless smile.

"No. Not for myself. How could I? I was but a *dog*, remember? Just a pet, with no hope of ever becoming anything more for you."

The way he said it extinguished the remnants of my anger.

"Did you ever wish to become something *more*?"

His chest expanded with a long breath. "For the longest time, I'd been content with my life, just the way it was. I saw you every day. I spent every night with you. It was enough. Things started to change only recently."

"What things?"

He drew me closer, resting his chin on the top of my head. I could no longer see his face in this position, and I wondered if that was at least part of the reason why he did it.

"Lately, I started noticing things about you that I never paid much attention to before."

"Like what?"

"Like how good you look in your workout clothes. Or how you moan in your sleep sometimes."

I twirled a finger in the soft, white fur on his chest. "I—I had no idea you paid attention to anything at all. I undressed in front of you all the time. I went to the bathroom with the door open."

"So did I." He chuckled softly.

My memories took off into embarrassing territory.

"I brought my friends in the bathroom when you were using it. I was so proud to show them what a smart dog you were. You knew how to use the toilet and even learned how to flush." I groaned, burying my face in his chest. "I'm so, so sorry, Maxx. It never occurred to me to concern myself with your privacy. Or...so many other things I did when you were around. It's mortifying to think about all of them now."

Like me clipping my toenails, or scratching my butt, or picking my nose. I never thought twice about doing any of those things when Pumpkin was around.

My face turned hotter and hotter with every new thing I recalled.

He laughed, soothingly rubbing my back. "Okay, but how many times did I lick my butt in your presence?"

"A lot!" I giggled.

"And I puked all over your bed that one time, remember? After your twelfth birthday party."

"Yeah, because my friends and I wanted you to celebrate with us and fed you a giant piece of cake. We figured since it wasn't chocolate, you should be fine."

"I would've been fine if I stopped after eating only a half of it. The piece was almost as big as me back then. And it tasted so good, I ate it all."

"It wasn't just the puking." I scrunched my nose, remembering that night in every stinking detail. "The farts were unbearable. I ended up sleeping on the balcony."

"It didn't even occur to me to question why you let me have the bed instead of kicking *me* out on the balcony for the night. But why did you?"

"You were so sick. I didn't have the heart to move you. But," I added with a smile, "neither did I want to sleep in the same room with you without a gas mask that night."

He smiled, too. There was warmth in his expression as we talked about us living and growing up together. There was absolutely no embarrassment or judgment on his part. And it put me at ease, too. He might look different, but there was still so much of my Pumpkin in him. We'd shared a life together.

He tightened his arms around me, and I leaned closer into his body.

"I'm so confused about you," I said, pressing my cheek to his chest.

"Why?"

"You're clearly a man now. But all my memories of you are from the time when you were Pumpkin. For ten years, I thought of you as my dog... It messes with my head now."

"It doesn't have to."

I released a sigh. "Who are you, Maxx? Who are you to me?"

"A friend," he said simply. "Always was. Always will be."

A friend.

That was easy. And so very true. It didn't matter how he looked or what his name was. He'd always been my closest friend.

Chapter 9

Cassy

There was a problem with Maxx being my friend, and *only* my friend. Friends didn't kiss, did they? They didn't have sexy dreams about each other, either. And they certainly wouldn't be sitting by the bathroom door while their friend was taking a shower, listening to the sound of running water and fantasizing about what it would be like to share the shower with him.

After we'd returned to the cabin and had lunch, I'd taken a shower first. It had a convenient blow dry feature that dried the water from hair and skin at the end. Once I'd finished and it was Maxx's turn, I started wondering if I could possibly wash and dry my clothes in the shower. Or I could hang them out to dry overnight. But that would mean I'd have to sleep naked.

And then my thoughts took an unexpected turn. Now, I was wondering if Maxx would still want to share the bed with me at night. Now that he'd changed, he might prefer more space, without my legs and arms draped all over him. That would be a problem if he did, as I realized I really liked draping my legs and arms all over him, no matter what form he was in. Though, this last form of his seemed exceptionally appealing in so many ways.

The sexy thoughts provided a distraction. They helped me not to dwell on the horrors of being trapped on a haunted spaceship with no crew. But they also made me anxious in a different way. I felt restless and unfocused, my attention on the sound of the water running behind the shower door, then on the noise of the dryer going off.

The door to the bathroom slid open, and Maxx stepped out. With one hand, he was still fluffing the fur around his neck. Somehow, that looked both cool and adorable. And it made me want to run my fingers through the white softness around his neck.

Stopped by my stare, he paused just past the doorway. Our eyes met, and my breath hitched. The silence grew heavier the longer we stared at each other.

"This is weird," I said, just to break the silence. "Weird to see you after a bath when I wasn't the one who gave it to you."

He tilted his head. With his pointy ears standing up, the gesture proved way too cute. "Would you have loved to bathe me?"

His expression remained earnest, except for a tiny spark of amusement deep inside his eyes.

"Well...um..." His question rendered me speechless. I had the answer to it, but I didn't feel ready to share it with him. Lost for words, I just reached for the white fur on his neck. "May I touch it?"

I used to love petting Pumpkin after washing him. His fur had been exceptionally soft and fragrant.

Stepping closer, Maxx rolled back his shoulders, giving me full access.

"Go ahead." He smiled. "Pet to your heart's content."

I sank my fingers into his warm, fragrant fur. It was still just a little bit damp and felt very much like Pumpkin's. The muscle structure under the fur, however, was different.

I traced his collarbone all the way to his shoulder, then slid my hand down the side of his chest. Just like his shoulders, the outer part of his chest was fur-free. The tips of my fingers glided along his warm, smooth skin that stretched over the hard muscles underneath.

As I reached his abdomen, he inhaled a sharp breath and gripped my wrist.

"Cassy." His voice sounded raspy and deeper than usual. "If you go any further..."

It came as a warning. But I was tempted to ignore it. I wished to keep exploring his body that was such an amazing mix of things, both familiar and new to me.

I wondered what it would feel like if his fingers were to explore my body, too. With a quick breath in, I raised my eyes to his. His long eyelashes, the color of dark chocolate, shaded his eyes, making them look darker, too. One turned hunter-green, the other was now the color of the stormy ocean.

He always had the most amazing eyes in any form he'd taken. Only before, their look never made me feel like how I did right now. My skin pricked with awareness in the wake of his gaze sliding down my body. The air in the room seemed to heat up. I didn't know what to do about it, only that I had to do something,

Holding his gaze, I lifted my hand to the zipper in front of my sports bra and pulled it open.

"Fuck," he groaned.

His eyes flashed. I took a step back, and he followed. He moved faster than me, closing the distance between us. He wrapped his arms around me.

"Cassy," he whispered, pressing his lips to the side of my face.

My heart sped up.

"I...I dreamed about you, Maxx, the way you are now. But I dreamed of you days ago. Before you...changed. Why?"

He trailed his kisses along my jawline. "I don't know. But this certainly feels like a dream."

He found my lips with his. His kiss was more confident now than the one before, more urgent, too. I parted my lips for him, and his tongue promptly invaded my mouth as if it was his right all along.

Both bunk beds were put away. Without breaking the kiss, he walked me backwards until my ass hit the table. One warm palm of his slid up my side. He flicked my open bra away and covered my breast with his hand.

I breathed faster, gasping softly against his mouth. He lifted me onto the table. I leaned back, propped up on my arms, as he kissed down to my chest, then sucked a nipple in.

Desire rolled through me, pooling hot in my lower belly. My thighs trembled. I gripped the side of the table as he kissed down my body. His tails wrapped around my ankles with a soft caress. He pulled my pants and underwear off. Then the fur around his neck tickled between my legs, and I grabbed his ears, stopping him from going any further.

"I've never gone this far," I rasped in confession.

He lifted his eyes to mine, flashing me a cocky grin.

"I know. I made sure of that."

That was a clear reference to my non-existent love life and the reminder that *he* was the main reason for it being non-existent in the first place. It should make me angry or at least irritated. Except that at that very moment, he pressed his chin to my most intimate spot, still grinning at me. Heat surged up my body.

Turning his head, he kissed the inner part of my thigh. The press of his lips was so gentle, so intimate. My reaction to it was more than physical. My heart swelled with emotion.

"Maxx..." I sank my fingers into the fur on his head. He parted me with his tongue, dragging it slowly.

The sensation was new and so intense, I whimpered. No one had touched me there before, other than myself. The caress of his mouth and tongue on me was an exquisite, incomparable experience. Warmth spread through me. Pressure throbbed hot where his tongue connected with my body. Lost to pleasure, I forgot where we were. All problems temporarily melted in the heat coursing through my body.

The achy pressure built higher with every swirl of his tongue inside me. He alternated tiny nibbles with gentle sucking, and it all created different sensations that blended into an incredible mix of pure ecstasy.

"Oh... God..." I pressed my feet into his shoulders, lifting my hips. "I'm..."

I forgot what I was going to say. Pleasure crested, rolling through me with the best orgasm ever. It robbed me of words. He gripped my hips, chasing every little shudder of my climax with his tongue.

I lay on the table, spent. He pulled himself up my body, leaving a trail of tiny, gentle kisses on my skin. When he reached my neck, I threw my arms around him.

"I've never... Maxx. This was... What was that? Where did you learn how to do that?"

He chuckled, kissing my face.

"I've done some research."

"What kind of research, this time? Did you watch sex videos or something? Porn?"

"That too. But I found porn not very helpful. It's not the best resource for researching the topic of female pleasure, you know?"

Sinking my hands into his fur, I lifted his head to see his face.

"Tell me, why did you research that topic in the first place?"

He propped himself up on his arms, lifting his torso off me.

"Out of general interest, at first. Sex is such a big part of human life, it's impossible to avoid learning about it while studying humans. But lately... Well, lately I searched for answers about what was happening to my body. To me. Physically and emotionally."

"And did you find the answers?"

"Some." He glanced aside. "Things aren't simple when you are the only one of your kind on the entire planet. Possibly in the entire Universe."

Compassion pinched my heart. Talk about being different. Maxx was going through multiple, incredible transformations, with no guidance from anyone.

I smoothed his fur and stroked his pointy ears.

"Is it scary to change forms this dramatically? You went from walking on four legs to walking on two. From making hardly any noise to talking." I slid a glance down his chest. "Your body changed overnight."

"It's unsettling, at first. And confusing. It was like an eruption of vastly different sensations in many parts of my body, some I didn't even know I had."

I hooked an arm around his shoulders, sitting up, and he straightened to give me space.

"Which of those sensations are you feeling right now?"

He heaved a breath. "So many of them. But most of all... Most of all, I just want to fuck you. As hard as they do in those porn videos."

I exhaled a husky laugh. This was brutally honest on his part. And it made me both nervous and intrigued.

"Do you?" I tipped my head down, avoiding his eyes as my cheeks heated. "And do you have all the...um, necessary *parts* for that?"

I skimmed my hand down his torso, but he grabbed my wrist again the moment my fingers reached the orange fur between his thighs.

"I do have...something," he said softly. "But it's different from that of humans. Do you understand?"

I curled my fingers as he held my hand at a safe distance from him.

"Well. I'd only ever seen the human part once or twice—"

"You have? When?"

I lifted my head and was met with his frown.

"Yes, *pumpkin*," I said with a hefty dose of sarcasm. "Your cyber security isn't as foolproof as you might've thought. I did manage to see a guy's dick, despite your best efforts."

I had a rule: no sex on a first date. And I hadn't broken it. But on a couple of occasions, a making-out session had gone far enough for me not to be completely ignorant about what a man's dick looked like.

"I never tried to keep you away from sex," he said. "Just away from a heartache."

In that, he had succeeded. Since that one betrayal in high school, I hadn't cried over a man ever again. But that was also because I learned my lesson not to trust a guy too quickly.

"Are you trying to distract me?" I wiggled my fingers, as he still held my wrist in his hand. "Because it's not working. I still want to see it."

He moved his jaw, clearly torn between letting me touch him and keeping me away.

"I promise, I won't freak out, whatever it is you have, okay?" I said earnestly, then added with a smile, "Promise not to laugh, either."

He rolled his eyes at me, and I giggled. Leaning in, I kissed his cheek.

"Come on, Maxx," I coaxed. "Let me touch you, please. I know you're dying to have my hands on you."

He didn't argue with the last statement but kept my hand firmly trapped. My other hand remained free, but I wasn't going to touch him without his explicit permission.

He brought his mouth to my ear. "Cassy, I have *three* tails."

"I know. And I like them."

The soft, feather-like caress of his tails skimmed up my legs.

"I know you're different, Maxx. But I like that about you. You're unique. Trust me, it doesn't matter what your dick looks like—"

"*Dicks.*"

"What?"

He placed his chin on my shoulder, hiding his face from me. "Three tails. Three cocks, Cassy."

"Oh," was all I could say.

He let go of my wrist, and I just wrapped both my arms around his middle, no longer going for his crotch.

Three?

Three...

That needed some time to absorb.

"How does it work?" I asked tentatively.

"I don't know. I've never had a chance to use them."

"Right. Well, are they..." I had so many questions. How big was each? Were they positioned in a line or in a cluster? Did he come from all of them at once or each demanded individual attention? And why *three?* Why?

However, there was a point in the saying *"A picture is worth a thou-sand words."*

"One or three, I still want to see. And touch," I said firmly.

With a deep breath, he leaned back a little. "All right. Go ahead."

His lips pinched, his features froze, his body tensed. Despite his permission, he clearly was nervous.

"It's okay, Maxx. It's just me, remember? You don't have to stress about me."

I moved a hand from his back to his front and dipped just the tips of my fingers into the thick fur between his thighs. I kept them hovering, giving him space, ready to withdraw completely at the slightest sign of him changing his mind. Instead, a touch met me.

Three prehensile appendages reached for my hand from the soft nest of his fur. They curled around my fingers, caressing my palm. Each was thicker than my thumb and almost twice as long as my hand.

Placing my head on Maxx's shoulder, I watched them undulate around my hand. They felt firm when I stroked one, but flexible. Tapered toward the end like tentacles. Smooth, with the veins bulging out slightly. And yes, they grew in a cluster, positioned close together at the base.

"Fascinating..." I let the taut appendages run between my fingers. Their skin felt especially silky to the touch, slicked by a thin sheen of lubrication. "That's so neat," I marveled.

Too absorbed by my exploration, I forgot to pay attention to anything else. Maxx's strangled gasp snapped me back to reality.

"Cassy. I...I can't..." He blew out a sharp breath.

His three cocks curled around each other. Pressed together, they formed something like a tight, thick rope. The rope convulsed. Once, twice. Then, a clear, gel-like substance shot out.

"God... Fuck..." Maxx panted as the "rope" in my hand undulated, releasing more of the clear substance, spurt after spurt.

A pleasant fragrance filled the air. It smelled like cinnamon and nutmeg with a hint of ginger, bringing to mind my mom baking pies in the fall.

I stroked along Maxx's "rope" one more time, making him shudder and moan as if in both pleasure and pain. He propped his hands on the table on either side of me and buried his face in my neck. I raked the fingers of my clean hand through the fur on the back of his head.

"Well, that didn't take long," he groaned.

"But was it all you thought it would be?" I asked, uncertain.

In addition to being no expert in any of this, I feared I'd gotten too distracted by my curiosity, playing with his body instead of paying attention to his pleasure.

He breathed hard against my shoulder. Worry wormed its way inside me. This was his first orgasm, and I had no idea if I managed to make it a good one for him.

Finally, he lifted his head.

"They don't do sex justice," he said with that dimply smile of his.

"Who are *they?*"

The smile twinkled in his eyes, too. "The porn videos. Sex in them doesn't look nearly as good as it feels."

I released a breath of relief. "So, you liked it?"

"Loved it!" He grabbed me from the table and took me in a twirl around the room. "Let's do it again."

I laughed. "Hey, hold your horses. We have stuff to do. It's not like we're on holiday here. At least let me wash my hand."

"Your hand?" He stopped twirling and set me down.

I waved the hand covered with his release between us. "It smells nice, though. I have to admit."

He squinted his eyes at the clear gel on my hand. "What is it?"

"You tell me." I shrugged. "It came out of *your* body."

"It doesn't look like the semen of the men in the videos."

"No. It doesn't smell like theirs, either. I'm sure men would get far more blowjobs if their stuff smelled this yummy." I brought my hand closer to my nose.

Maxx grabbed my arm and dragged me toward the sink. "Wash it off. Quickly."

The smile disappeared from his face, giving place to a worried expression. His concern filtered through to me.

"What's going on?" I asked as he stuck my hand under the faucet and scraped my hand clean in the running water.

"I wasn't *born*, Cassy. I was *made*. For a very specific purpose, it seems."

Extermination, lethal...

Some of the words from his number rose in my mind.

"I don't know why this particular function was added to my design in this form," he continued. "It may be meant for something other than procreation. In either case, it's best not to have it in contact with your skin for long."

Mixed with the gel, the water in the sink gained a shimmer. I watched it twirl before disappearing down the drain. So much remained unexplained about Maxx, but the reason for his existence seemed to be clear to him—violence.

He'd been protecting me from others all his life. And now, he was trying to protect me from himself.

Chapter 10

Maxx

"Stay close." He squeezed Cassy's hand.

She didn't need the reminder, clinging to him like a drowning woman to a lifesaver as they walked through the corridors to the elevator.

After their exploration that morning and using everything Cassy had told him about this place, he'd been drafting a map of the ship in his head. By now, he could reasonably narrow down the location of the main controls, and that was where they were heading.

Gripping his hand, Cassy constantly glanced back over her shoulder. He knew she was terrified. The visions she'd encountered on this ship bothered her. He didn't know what they were, but as long as they presented no direct threat, he was happy to ignore them.

"No ghosts," he said cheerfully, trying to calm her down.

"Not yet," she breathed out.

They took the elevator to the main floor. Cassy took a long breath before entering the large room with giant windows. She glanced at one briefly, then dropped her gaze to their joint hands.

"Being here makes me feel so small."

Staring into the open space unsettled something inside him, too. Instead, he tried to keep his attention on the path straight ahead.

After crossing the room, they walked along a wide, short corridor that led them to a set of double doors. These were taller and wider than the doors in the lower levels. The walls here were a lighter gray rather than black like below.

Cassy pushed at the doors with no result. They were locked.

"Do you think it's here?" she asked.

"I'm positive." Logic dictated it should be the main control room, but of course he had no way of knowing for sure. He sensed, however, that Cassy felt calmer when he acted with confidence.

He splayed his hand on the door, searching for the lock screen. It lit up on contact, taking up almost half of the entire surface of the door.

"Wow!" Cassy took a step back. "That's a big one."

Prompts flashed in green and blue. They then quickly changed to red, blocking his access. He focused harder, trying to break through the wall that kept him out of the system.

"Dammit..." It wouldn't budge.

"No luck?" Cassy asked sympathetically.

"No. This one is blocked."

"Okay." She unzipped the pouch on her belt. "Let me try it my way."

She produced her keys from the pouch. Before he had a chance to wonder how her keys could help in this situation, she stabbed the screen with the spike on her keychain.

"Dad gave it to me, remember?" She kept hitting the screen, smashing it to pieces. "He meant for me to use it for self-defense in case I ran into some asshole one day. But since you've been keeping all assholes—and all men in general—away from me anyway..." she gave him a look over her shoulder, then continued breaking the screen. "Well, it came in handy this way."

The remnants of the screen hung on the door in a mess of glass and wires. Pieces of see-through panels fell out as Cassy scooped out the rest.

"If it's anything like the cabin doors below," she murmured, digging through the remaining tangle of glass and plastic, "then there should be a deadbolt here on the edge somewhere."

Her brow knitted into a frown as she kept searching.

"Is there a problem?" he asked.

"Yeah… They have it blocked off here." She withdrew her hand from the door and stepped back. "There is only smooth metal, like a bar placed in front of the deadbolts."

"Let me see." He stuck his hand in.

The bar ran inside the door along its edge. It was thick and seemed solid. He gripped it with his fingers and yanked. It wouldn't move.

Cassy touched his arm gently. "Let's think of something else."

"No. Wait." He closed his eyes.

Something stirred inside him. A presence that had been largely foreign to him before. Lately, it'd risen to the surface twice. Both had happened at the time of crises and without any conscious effort on his part.

When Cassy had been attacked in the park, the mysterious power had sprung to the surface from deep within him. It had made him stronger, faster, and much more vicious, too.

The second time, it'd happened when he was locked in the darkness and Cassy had freed him. That time, his fear and desperation might've been the trigger to chase her. Thankfully, he'd recognized her and was able to gain control over whatever it'd been.

Now, he called on that power himself. It answered his call eagerly. Energy surged through his muscles. His very bones buzzed with strength. His hand clamped into a fist. The metal in his hand compressed like cardboard. He yanked the bar out of the door, as if it was made of flimsy plastic not solid metal, and tossed it on the floor.

"Oh…" Cassy bent to pick the bar up. "Wow." Falling silent, she inspected the bent and dented metal.

He ran his fingers inside the door, searching for the deadbolt. There wasn't one but three of them. His body shook from all the currents running through him. He felt he could simply rip this door out without bothering with the locks. A part of him wished he'd do it. Break. Tear. Smash and crash. That dark presence begged to be unleashed. It threatened to take over.

"Maxx." Cassy's voice filtered as if from far away. She sounded so small, so vulnerable compared to the force raging inside him. "Your eyes are red. Just like before."

With his hand inside the door, he pressed his forehead to the cool metal surface of the panel.

"Are you alright?" she asked softly, stroking his arm.

Her touch made him wish both to grab and ravage her on the spot and to fall at her feet to beg her forgiveness for that urge.

He drew in a long breath, forcing the darkness to recede. Only when he felt like himself again, did he meet her concerned gaze.

"I'm good. It's fine, Cassy."

Her full, pretty lips formed a smile, looking irresistible. "Oh good. Your eyes are back to normal again."

Unable to resist, he leaned toward her and placed a soft kiss on her mouth. She gasped softly. A new twinkle appeared in her eyes when he pulled back.

She touched her lips briefly. "You're by far the best kisser I've ever met. Which is weird, since it doesn't even look like you care about a technique or anything."

He shrugged. "Does a kiss need a technique to be good?"

"Obviously, it doesn't." She lifted her arm, showing her forearm to him. "Look, I have goosebumps just from that little peck you gave me. You make me tingle all over and forget about everything."

Her words made him warm inside. The darkness melted away completely, leaving only bright sunshine in his chest.

"I don't have a technique." He grinned. "But if you'd like me to work on developing one, I'm more than happy to practice with you any time you wish."

"Smooth." She glanced aside, a shy smile playing on her delicious lips. "How about you open that door now, *pumpkin?*"

She said the last word in a teasing way, not as a name but a nickname. He was glad to have a different name for this new form of his.

But he still loved hearing that word from her. The familiarity of it made him smile wider.

He touched the deadbolts but couldn't quite get a grip on either of them to pull them out. Instead, he reached for that power inside him once again. Feeling much more in control now, he sent a small current down to his fingertips. They stuck to the end of the deadbolts. When he pulled, the smooth bars shifted, and the doors opened.

"Here you go." He shoved the two halves apart.

Lights flickered to life in the large, round room beyond. After the constant semi-darkness in the rest of the ship, the white and yellow lights here were blinding.

"Wow, these are bright!" Cassy threw an arm up, shielding her eyes from the light.

His vision adjusted to the new lighting instantaneously, however. He immediately surveyed the space, taking in the multiple control panels that lined the rounded walls and climbed up the columns between the windows.

He came up to the one in the middle and placed his hand on it. The panel lit up. But just like with the door lock before, he couldn't access the controls or get to the information beyond the readable prompts on the screen.

"And? Can you do it?" Cassy stepped to his side, staring at the screen, too.

He wished he had some good news for her, that he could tell her he'd bring her back home soon. But he couldn't lie to her.

He shook his head. "It's protected. I can't access the navigation system. Not yet, anyway."

There was still time for him to figure it out. The ship's life support system appeared to be functioning fine. The supplies in the food replicator would last for a while. If he worked on it...

"Would this help?" Cassy dangled her spiky keychain over the panel.

He laughed at her sudden love for destruction. "You're a menace."

She cocked a hip. "If you think it helps, I'll break everything inside this blasted ship."

"I won't allow you to continue causing damage to my ship," a voice unexpectedly informed them, coming from behind them.

Cassy yelped and gripped his arm. He whipped around toward the voice.

"The ghost," Cassy gasped as they faced the figure draped in white.

Chapter 11

Maxx

A slim figure dressed in white stood in the middle of the room. The bright light bounced off the pristine white cloak, making it shimmer. Inside its hood, the dark purple face stood in stark contrast to the crisp white of the cloak. Both the face and the figure had delicate lines and features that appeared feminine.

"Who are you?" Maxx took a step forward, placing himself between Cassy and the newcomer.

"My name is Anima," the person replied in an even voice that lacked any softness. "I am in charge of this ship."

Anima spoke in a language he'd never heard before coming here but understood without any difficulties—Ivodian. He recognized the voice, too. It was the same that had spoken to him before, back when he was locked in the darkness.

"What did she say?" Cassy asked in a half-whisper, peeking from around his arm. "Is she dead?"

"I'm neither dead nor alive," the woman replied, not sparing her a glance. She clearly understood Cassy but spoke in Ivodian.

"What is she saying?" Cassy's voice sounded high with approaching panic.

Maxx noted the subtle movement of the white shroud and the shimmer in its folds. He sensed the faint buzz of energy radiating from Anima and her connection to the ship. The image was a hologram, he realized, not a ghost.

"It's the ship's AI, Cassy," he explained in English. "Artificial intelligence that's the main operating system of this ship. That's what you are, aren't you, Anima?"

The purple lips curved into a barely visible smile. "Precisely, soldier. I am the brain of this spaceship. And I won't let you damage it."

He lifted both hands in a pacifying gesture. "I won't touch a thing around here if you just take us back to Earth and leave us in the park where you took us from."

The AI shook her head, making the ends of her spacious hood sway. "Going to Earth is no longer a part of my mission."

"What is your mission?"

"To return the missing unit to the base on Rimall."

Was he the *missing unit?* But what was Rimall?

He searched through his extensive memory and quickly found the answer. Rimall was one of the colonies of the planet Ivodi. Many decades ago, it used to hold a military base, but its size had been greatly reduced since. Now, there was just a frontier compound with a small research facility, a medical hospital, and a local law enforcement office.

The three moons of Rimall were significantly more populated, with one holding a luxury resort, and another one, named Us'ae being home to large estate properties.

"Why Rimall?" he asked, genuinely confused.

"That is the final destination of my mission."

Cassy clung to his side, her fingers digging into his arm in a death grip. But she kept silent, letting them talk.

"I am the 'unit' you're speaking of, right?" he asked the AI.

"Yes. The experimental model and the only one existing in its class."

"The only one?"

"There were four capsules created," Anima explained. "Two permanently stopped their development due to an error in their design. One was seized and decommissioned by the authorities. We managed to protect the last one. It was sent into outer space along a predetermined trajectory in hopes that it could be retrieved one day. Sadly, we lost the beacon signal in the proximity of the planet Earth seventy-three universal years ago. And only late last week, I sensed it again."

"In the park." It dawned on him. "I set something off that day, didn't I?"

The AI lowered her head in affirmation.

"The main beacon of the capsule was damaged upon arrival to the planet Earth, either during the entry into its atmosphere or on impact during the landing. Thankfully, the secondary beacon was activated the moment you accessed your core programming."

"In other words, when I got angry at Cassy's attacker," he muttered to himself, remembering the burning desire to be stronger in order to fight the thug who dared threaten his Cassy. He'd wished to annihilate the man on the spot, reaching deep into the darkness pulsing inside him—his core programming, as the AI had just put it. "Who sent you to get me?"

"My mission program comes directly from Professor Vrax and his team."

"Professor *who*?"

"The man who created you."

A trickle of apprehension rolled down his spine. "What is he going to do with me if he gets me back?"

"That is beyond the scope of my mission, which ends with my delivering you to him."

"Right." He glanced at Cassy, who kept watching them with her eyes opened wide with worry. "Take me to Rimall if you must," he said to the AI. "But bring Cassy back to Earth first."

"The female?" Anima swung her gaze to the woman at his side. "I have no use for her. She's a glitch in the execution of my mission."

"Then take her back to where you took her from." If Cassy was home, safe and sound, he could deal with whatever came his way. Sooner or later, he would find his way back to her.

A part of him actually wished to go wherever the ship would take him if that meant finally finding answers to the questions he'd had all his life. What exactly was he? Who created him and why? How could he gain the full control of his body and learn every hidden capability of it? What was his lifespan? And most importantly, how was he to live the rest of his life now, without inadvertently harming those he loved?

"Returning to Earth is not on my mission plan." The AI remained undeterred.

"Then, we'll have to put it on your plan." He wrapped his arm around Cassy's shoulders.

She glanced up at him with so much trust in her dark-brown eyes, it floored him. She hadn't understood a word of his conversation with the AI. But she looked ready to follow him wherever he went.

Cassy lifted her little spike again. "Is it time to smash things?"

This girl... Small but vicious. He hugged her tighter to him.

But smashing things could be their answer in this situation, after all. If he could find the right components to break, the ones that housed the AI, then he could work on finding access to the navigation system without the meddling of the lovely Anima.

"You will not damage my ship," Anima said in perfect English, clearly addressing Cassy this time.

Cassy gave him a questioning glance, as if waiting for him to point at the next place to stab with her spike.

"Since you refuse to lay the course back to Earth," he told the AI, "we'll have no choice but to find it ourselves."

"Then you're not leaving me a choice, either." The faint threatening note in the even voice of the AI sent a buzz of warning through his core.

He swept the room with his gaze, trying to determine where the threat would come from if she retaliated against them. He expected a spark, or a blast, or a weapon appearing from a hidden slot somewhere—something tangible.

Nothing like that came. Silence hung over the room as he searched for a hidden threat.

Finally, a soft hissing sound reached his hearing.

"What are you doing?" he demanded from Anima.

The hologram image of the Ivodian woman folded her arms.

"Like I said, I have no use for the female. It's not on my mission plan to bring her along, either dead or alive. And now, I choose to have her dead by the time of our arrival on Rimall."

She spoke in English for Cassy to understand.

"She wants to kill me?" Cassy's hand tightened on the spike, signaling she wouldn't give up without a fight. Only there was no visible threat to fight.

The faint hissing noise continued, bringing a perceptible change to the air in the room. Breathing suddenly got more and more difficult. Not just for him. Cassy's chest also rose and fell rapidly, laboring for every breath.

"What's happening?" She looked around wildly.

He leveled the AI with a glare. "You can't change the air. If you do, you'll kill me too. I need oxygen to breathe, just like humans do. If I die, your mission will fail."

Talking got harder, too. Cassy staggered, propping herself up against the console behind her. He drew her into his side for support.

Anima tilted her head. "You're not that easily killed, soldier. Your biological functions may slow down for the remainder of our journey. But you will survive. Your condition upon our arrival will be satisfactory for the successful completion of my mission."

Cassy slackened against his side. Her head lolled.

"Fuck you and your mission," he hissed through his teeth.

He lifted Cassy into his arms to stop her from collapsing to the floor.

"I will not allow you to sabotage my mission," the AI replied calmly. "If you resist, I will access your system directly again and—"

He had no time or desire to listen to that.

"You'd have to hardwire me for that. Good luck with that. I'll never let you come anywhere near me with those wires again."

With Cassy in his arms, he marched straight through the hologram on his way to the exit.

NOTHING IN HIS LIFE held any meaning if Cassy didn't survive this. Sprinting down the corridor of the lower level, he went through the steps of a plan to keep Cassy alive.

With the oxygen being rapidly sucked out of the ship, he had to find a way to replenish it. The solution was to make oxygen for her. The experiment Cassy once did at home with her dad leapt to his mind. She later presented it at a science fair in her school and won first place.

Using a battery, a glass of water, and two pencils, she'd split water into oxygen and hydrogen, with a touch of chloride gas as a by-product. The experiment had interested him enough back then that he'd researched quite a bit about how oxygen had been produced for space travel by humans before Voranians, the aliens from the planet Neron, shared their far more efficient technology with Earth.

He rushed into their cabin and kicked the door shut behind him, then opened the bunk bed. Carefully placing Cassy on the lower bunk, he kissed her forehead. Her eyes remained wide open, she struggled to say something. He cupped her face with his hands.

"Don't speak. We don't have air for it."

She nodded, her chest heaving in the struggle to breathe.

He decided to use just a little bit more of the precious oxygen to reassure her. "It'll be fine. I promise."

She nodded again. Unconditional trust shone in her eyes. She trusted him to keep her alive.

Moving swiftly, he found a big enough jar in a compartment above the sink. Opening the food replicator, he pulled two long tubes out of its dispenser mechanism. He'd fix that later. Right now, Cassy needed air to breathe far more than she needed food to eat.

After filling the jar with warm water from the tap, he dissolved some salt in it, then made a lid from a piece of plastic he ripped off a cabinet. He used one tube to filter the hydrogen and the chloride out of the jar and led it into the corridor outside of their cabin. He threaded it through the lock hole in the door and plugged the hole with a piece of the blanket from the bed to prevent the harmful gasses from seeping back into their room. The end of the oxygen tube he placed gently into one of Cassy's nostrils.

"Hold it," he whispered.

Her fingers trembled as she gripped the tube.

He had no graphite or batteries on hand, but he had his body. It was filled with an array of metals and minerals. And it was a battery on its own. His body was a machine capable of many wonders he'd learned, as long as he let his "core programming" take charge.

He inserted both arms into the holes he'd made in the lid and sank his hands into the water. Then he closed his eyes and let the darkness rise.

Somewhere deep in his mind, a source of knowledge and skills lay untouched. No one had taught him how to use it, but it was a part of him, nevertheless. If he just let his conscious part retreat, the rest had a chance to act.

A current coursed through his limbs. The right materials of his body were used. The water bubbled around his fingers, separating into gasses. He fisted the corresponding tubes, sending the life-saving oxygen Cassy's way.

She sucked the air in greedily. When their eyes met, her lips moved, forming the words, *"Thank you."*

He nodded, but his mind never stopped working. This was like fighting thirst with drops of water. She needed more oxygen, faster. His brain was already devising a plan on how to improve his makeshift device, make it work more efficiently.

The plan, however, didn't account for his own need for breathable air or for the possibility of the ship's ruthless AI shutting off the water just as it had shut off the oxygen supply.

How long would his own "biological parts" function without air? How long before he, too, collapsed? Breathless.

Chapter 12

Cassy

I won first place at a science fair once. It helped, of course, that the rest of the entries consisted of mostly soda-and-vinegar volcanoes. But I was ridiculously happy about my win. My dad was very proud, too.

I'd come up with the idea for my project after a long conversation with Dad. It started when I'd asked him how people breathed in his airplane. He told me about air processing. Then, the topic shifted to astronauts in a spaceship. And he told me all about getting oxygen out of water. He said we could try it at home, and of course I immediately wanted to do it.

We'd practiced the experiment in our kitchen, with Pumpkin dozing off in the armchair nearby. It would forever remain one of my fondest memories—spending time with my dad on one of his few days off.

Winning the science fair was a cherry on top of the most amazing cake of that experience. I was grinning so wide when accepting the ribbon, my mouth hurt all night. My school's principal shook my hand while someone snapped a picture of us.

I was so happy. The world seemed pink and yellow with purple bubbles floating by. I glanced back at the table with my experiment. There was a man standing next to it. His pointy ears looked so adorable that I giggled.

Instead of the graphite pencils, the man had his hands inserted into the jar of water. The jar was so much bigger than I remembered mine to be. The skin on his hands and wrists was ink black. And I wasn't sure if it was because of my experiment or if he was born that way.

Either way, he was the most handsome man I'd ever seen. Just looking into his blue-and-green eyes made me want to smile wider. My heart soared.

My entire body seemed to float, too.
Up...up I went like a purple bubble... Into the sky of pink and yellow...

"CASSY," A WOMAN'S VOICE called.

No one called me Cassy anymore, except for one person. But this wasn't his voice.

"Cassy, can you open your eyes, please?"

Could I? I tried. My eyelids felt so heavy, I almost gave up right away. But they cracked open after a while, letting soft yellow light in.

"Who are you?" I tried to focus on the white-and-purple blob in front of me.

"My name is Doctor Luvai," the woman said. She sounded kind but unfamiliar.

"A doctor? Am I sick?"

"Yes. You were very sick, Cassy. But you're getting better. Your condition is stable."

"What was it? What did I have? The flu?" For some reason, this was the only sickness I could think of. My head remained fuzzy.

"Um...no," the doctor said. "It wasn't a viral infection. You suffered from dehydration, hypoxia, exhaustion, hypothermia..."

"Hypothermia? But I'm not cold." None of the other words she'd said made sense to me. Maybe because my brain was still waking up as she spoke. By the last word, it had awoken enough to comprehend it.

The blurry outline of the woman standing over me nodded. "Not anymore. We had to put you into a recovery capsule until your vital signs had stabilized."

I closed my eyes again. "I want my mom. Is she here?"

Mom had always been close when I got sick. And I really needed someone close to me right now.

"No," the woman sounded sympathetic. "But we confirmed your identity with Earth, using your biological material, Cassy." Her voice lifted. "Your parents have been notified of your location and condition."

My location...

I remembered the park, the flying saucer, and the haunted ship. I was no longer on Earth. Though *where* exactly I was remained a question.

I opened my eyes again, finally able to focus on her face. It was bright purple. Alarm zapped through me. I shrank away from her to the very edge of the weird bed I lay in.

"There is no reason to worry," she said soothingly, stretching a hand to me in a calming gesture. "You're safe."

"Safe?" I narrowed my eyes at her as my vision finally cleared.

The woman was wearing white coveralls instead of the cloak, but her image had the same ethereal quality. It shimmered and shifted, like a ghost.

I went to slap her outstretched hand away from me, but my fingers went right through it. She looked like a ghost, but Maxx had told me she was a hologram.

"You're the AI."

"No." She shook her head. "I'm a real person. Only I work remotely due to health reasons. You're at the hospital on Rimall—"

"Stop with your lies," I cut her off. "You tried to kill Maxx and me. Where is Maxx? What did you do to him?"

Her blue eyes widened. "Who is Maxx? And who tried to kill you?"

I sat up in the narrow bed that looked more like a padded lower part of a coffin with raised edges. I had a long shirt on and a pair of loose pants. Both were white, just like the woman's coveralls and the walls of the room we were in. The only colors came from the window that opened onto a wall of green and purple vines with multi-colored flowers.

I gripped the edge of my bed, trying to figure out the best way to climb out of it.

"Careful." The woman kept holding out her hand, as if she could stop me with her hologram limbs.

A bundle of see-through filaments dangled from my arm and chest. Their other ends were connected to a wall of screens behind me.

The woman threw a worried look at the screens. "Please remain in the capsule, for your own safety. You've been exposed to both the lack of oxygen and an overabundance of it. Both have taken a toll on your body."

I crossed my arms over my chest. "I won't do a damn thing unless I see Maxx right now. What did you do to him?"

A panel in the wall across from my capsule-bed slid open, and a man walked in. He was tall, wearing similar white coveralls as the hologram woman. His face and hands were purple, too, only of a slightly less saturated shade than hers.

"Doctor Luvai, please forgive the interruption," he said politely, "but I think the patient may find an in-person interaction more preferable at this time."

Like the woman, he also had no hair on his head. Seven long, slim, hairless tails undulated behind each of them. A row of piercings shaped as semi-circles ran up the bridge of the man's nose to the middle of his forehead.

Judging by the purple skin color and the tails, both the woman and the man were Ivodians.

"You're not a hologram?" I stared at him.

He walked around the image of the doctor, rather than going right through her, which was a sign of respect, I assumed.

"No. I'm not a hologram." He stretched his hand to me. "I'm Professor Xez, from the Arlex Research Facility on Ivodi. I arrived on Rimall while you were recuperating.

He certainly looked more solid than the slim, petite doctor. A small paunch of his belly protruded over the belt of his overalls.

His handshake was firm.

"Did I get the Earth greeting right?" he asked, looking rather pleased with himself. "The handshake seemed to be the most common one when I looked it up."

"Yeah. It is, I think." I couldn't stop staring at him. It was my first time meeting an alien in person. If I didn't count Maxx, of course. But Maxx didn't really count since he came from Pumpkin. He might be from another planet, but we grew up together. He was my closest friend.

Something inside my chest tightened painfully without him at my side. In one form or another, Maxx had been with me most of my life. Since I brought him to our apartment, it'd been a rare night that we didn't spend together. I missed him, and it hurt more than the lack of oxygen had hurt.

"Will you tell me where Maxx is?" I asked the professor.

"I assume you're talking about the M.A.X.X. unit we've found on the spaceship with you?"

The letters in Maxx's name came through as words when he said them. Only now I realized that neither the doctor nor the professor spoke English to me. By the sound of it, they both spoke the same language as the AI of the haunted ship did—Ivodian. The language I didn't know, but the meaning of their words was conveyed to my brain seamlessly.

"Did I..." I touched behind both my ears, searching for bumps and scars. A spot on the left side of my skull felt a bit sore. "Did you implant a translator into my head? Without my consent?"

"It's for your own good, really—" Doctor Luvai started but stopped, met with my glare.

The professor obviously didn't get it as he kept talking, "The implantation surgery is practically risk free. All over the galaxy, translators are implanted from birth. Earth is the only planet falling behind on that."

"That's not the point," I protested. "You performed a surgery on me without asking if I wanted to have it."

"Cassy, don't you want the benefit of understanding us?" He moved a chair from the wall to my capsule-bed and sat in it. "Doctor Luvai and her team have performed several procedures on you without having a way to ask for your consent. If they didn't operate, you'd be dead."

I turned to face Doctor Luvai, torn between feeling angry at and grateful to her and her team. They must've pumped a whole bunch of weird alien drugs into me. My mood seemed to swing on some wild pendulum from hell. My mind had a hard time catching up.

"Well..." She clasped her hands together in front of her. "I think I should give you some privacy to...um, let Professor Xez explain things... Or to answer whatever questions you may have."

"Thank you, Doctor." The professor nodded, and the hologram instantly dissipated into the air.

I rubbed my forehead, trying to collect my thoughts. Unfortunately, the professor wouldn't shut up.

"Historically, Ivodian women are physically much weaker than our men," he chatted. "Our females are cherished and protected. They suffer from poor health all their lives and often work from home, remotely, like Doctor Luvai. Although, that may change in the near future. We've been researching ways to improve their wellbeing, and there was a significant breakthrough in that area recently."

"I'm glad to hear that," I said distractedly. This sounded like good news for Ivodi, but my focus was all over the place right now. "Am I really on another planet?"

"Yes. This is not Earth, I assure you. Rimall has been colonized by Ivodi for centuries. It's not the best planet to inhabit due to its hostile wildlife. We couldn't improve the conditions here without risking destroying its entire ecosystem, which is too unique to destroy. But Rimall's three moons are lovely. They make this area one of the most popular vacation destinations. The resorts are excellent. And Us'ae has the most luxurious estate properties in the galaxy."

I stopped the talkative professor by raising a hand. "That's fascinating, Professor. But why am I here?"

"You arrived on a spaceship that has been listed as missing for over seven decades. It was thought to be lost in space shortly before the military base at this very location was dismantled. It used to house a military research facility. The work of the scientists here brought us many technological advances that greatly improved our space travel. Do you know that Ivodians are historically a race of conquerors and explorers?"

"No. I didn't know that."

The professor clearly took my confession as an invitation to explain. He sat up straighter and launched into a lecture.

"Ivodi has the largest number of colonies in the galaxy. Our own planet has only a small portion of habitable land and is overpopulated. Since the discovery of space travel, we've been focusing on improving both our technology in that area and the skills of our warriors."

"Warriors? Are there any wars going on around here?"

"Not currently. Officially, Ivodi isn't at war with any sentient beings right now. A vast majority of our colonies are void of life. But colonization and exploration often are as demanding as wars in terms of technology and manpower—"

I cut him off again by raising a hand.

"I'm sorry. All of this is truly interesting. But I just can't see how any of it has anything to do with Maxx and me."

"Oh but it does," he assured me. "The unit you're referring to as Maxx was created right here at this very facility, back when this station was under the jurisdiction of the Army."

"Maxx was made here?"

"Yes. Parts of the technology that lie at the base of his design are still being used in all our spaceships and some of our weapons. Except that his creators decided to take it further. By splicing biological characteristics of several sentient species and genetic material of selected animals and including the latest technology of the time, they created what they hoped would turn into a super species."

"Why? What did they want him to do?"

The man shrugged. "To fight, more effectively than several men. To explore, by going where no living being could. Apparently, there were also a few lesser-known plans to sell or rent the units as missionaries for interplanetary governments at war."

"They wanted him to be a super soldier?"

The professor nodded. "Among many other things. However, when our government recognized the potentially dire consequences of cyborg experiments, the production of these units was outlawed and ordered to be stopped."

"Only they didn't stop, did they?"

"Most did. But a few of the group chose to ignore the orders, including the head of the research, Professor Vrax. They created four prototypes but claimed that there were only three. Two failed early. One was surrendered to the authorities and decommissioned. But the fourth one was sent off the planet to hide it. The group intended to recover the unit when it would be safer to do so. However, they failed to find it. Until now, it seems."

"So, they sent that haunted spaceship after Maxx?"

"Why haunted?" He blinked at me in confusion.

"Never mind." I waved him off. "It was unmanned, with only the AI running it. Kind of like a Flying Dutchman in space."

"I'm sorry, your reference got lost in translation this time." He touched behind his ear where his translator implant must be located.

"It doesn't matter. My point is, it had no crew."

The professor perked up. "Oh, it couldn't have any crew, of course. The people who operated it, as well as those who sent it, are long dead."

"They died? But why?"

"From old age. It was so long ago, and they weren't that young to begin with when it all happened. But the ship kept going through space with one mission in its programming, to recover the missing M. A. X. X. unit and return it to the base, even though the base was no longer there. So, it brought you here. And just in time, it seemed. We found you unconscious in one of the passenger cabins. The missing unit was with you, also in a dire condition. There was a severe lack of breathable air on the ship and no running water. We're still unclear what he was trying to do with you. Was he the one who harmed you? Or was he trying to revive you?"

I brought a hand to my throat, remembering how I struggled for every breath as Maxx rushed me through the corridors of the spaceship. I recalled him doing something at the sink. I'd had a dream or a hallucination of my science fair project. Somehow, he'd re-created the experiment. He'd made oxygen for me to breathe.

"He kept me alive," I said.

"Incredible." The professor was staring at me, but I had a feeling he didn't really see me, stunned by what I'd just said.

"Please tell me where Maxx is," I begged. "Is he okay?"

His focus sharpened, returning to me. "You wish to know the unit's condition?"

"I wish to know if my friend is well. Has he been fed, taken care of? Is he happy?"

"Your *friend? Happy?* But he's a machine."

I fisted my hands, calling on my patience. "Maxx is a person in everything that counts. I need to see him." I grabbed the edge of my capsule-crib. "Can you help me out of this thing, or do I have to figure it out on my own?"

"Doctor Luvai hasn't authorized your leaving the capsule yet."

"Well, that's too bad. But if you don't let me see Maxx, I'll have to go search for him myself."

I lifted a leg over the padded border of the capsule. In the process, I must have yanked at the wires sticking out of me because one of the screens blinked and something beeped.

The professor leaped to his feet, his expression alarmed. "Please, I beg you, stay where you are."

I kept my leg up like a dog by a water hydrant, making it clear my staying put was my negotiation point. "Where is Maxx?"

The professor pinched the bridge of his nose then ran his fingers up and down the vertical row of silver piercings in the middle of his forehead.

"He's been detained and secured," he finally said.

"What?" I plopped back on my ass. "You arrested him? But why? He hasn't done anything wrong."

"Well, you see his mere existence is a crime. He never should've been made in the first place."

"But it happened. He's here now. He exists. And he's a living, breathing person."

"*Breathing,* yes. But he's not considered a living being. Neither is he a person—"

A wail of a siren ripped through the air. I jerked, drawing my legs up, instinctively making myself smaller.

"What's happening?"

The professor turned to face the window then the door.

"A wall breach?" He sounded uncertain.

"*Attention. Attention,*" a mechanical voice blasted through the speakers somewhere. "*A dangerous element escaped its confinement. The main level is in lockdown, starting immediately. Keep clear of the atrium area. The security unit has been dispatched.*"

"What's happening?" I repeated.

"*A dangerous element...*" the professor muttered under his breath. "I bet I know who that is."

"Maxx?"

"*Attention. Attention...*" the voice continued.

Then, a long, deafening roar rolled through the building. It was blood-curdling and terrifying. Only it failed to scare me. Instead of cowering, I threw my leg over the edge of the damn crib-capsule and climbed out. The wires popped out of my skin one by one, making the screens scream and flash.

"Cassy? Where are you going?" Professor Xez yelled. Standing in the middle of the room, he looked torn between tending to the screens, running for the door, and stopping me.

I paused, giving him a suspicious stare.

"How do you know my name, Professor? Did Maxx tell you?" Even if they confirmed my identity with Earth, they would have the name Cassidy. Cassy could've come only from Maxx.

He shook his head. "I haven't had a chance to speak to him yet."

"Did you search his memories, then?"

"We needed to assess the danger he represents."

"So, you snooped inside his head, instead of simply speaking to him?" They took no time to get to know him, instead they treated him as a machine right away. And now, they questioned his right to exist.

"Cassy, wait—"

I lifted a finger, pointing it at his chest. "It's *Cassidy* to you."

I slid the door open and ran out into the hallway.

Chapter 13

Cassy

I ran through the spacious white corridor.

"Atrium. Main floor," the announcement had said.

What floor was I on?

"Cass... Cassidy!" the professor yelled behind me. The sound of his heavy footsteps boomed not that far away.

I ran right, then took a left turn. There were signs with directions on every corner. But as great as the translator implant was for spoken language, it was no help when it came to the written one.

Another roar reverberated through the corridors, and I followed the sound.

"Maxx!" I screamed. "Where are you?"

He roared again. It sounded so close.

I turned around a corner and came onto a long balcony with a glass railing. It circled around the open space that stretched down for several floors below. There was an indoor garden on the lowest level. Slim, feather-like trees grew in decorative planters. A milky-colored creek trickled between the rocks laid along a path, ending in a fountain in the middle of the room.

My red-eyed beast stood on all fours by the creek, his three tails lashing wildly against his hind paws. Maxx had taken his most terrifying form.

No one was around him. He was all alone. Tossing his head back, his long fangs bared, he released another deafening roar.

"I'm here, Maxx!" I leaned over the railing.

His red eyes met mine the moment a group of armed Ivodians rushed into the atrium garden. They formed a circle around him, aiming their weapons at him.

My worry spiked into panic.

"Maxx!"

He crouched on his hind paws and...jumped. Like a released spring, his body stretched in the air. His tails spread behind him. He soared, covering the distance of all the floors between us. I leaped back from the railing, and he landed on top of me, knocking me to the ground.

His weight was off me, but his front paws pressed my shoulders into the rubbery floor of the balcony. His bared fangs glistened in the bright light. He breathed heavily, his red eyes unfocused.

I refused to be intimidated by him, regardless of what appearance he happened to have.

"It's me, Maxx. You know that. We've been through this before. You don't scare me, *pumpkin*. I know you way too well to be scared of you, no matter how much you glare at me with those red eyes of yours."

I reached for his face and scratched his cheek.

"Do you still like belly rubs?" I smiled.

He leaned into my touch.

"Of course you do," I murmured, smoothing down the massive mane around his neck.

His lips quivered and relaxed, hiding his teeth. With a soft click, his jaw shrank, and it didn't stop shrinking. His elongated face shifted into a man's face right in front of my eyes. His claws retreated, the paws changing into hands. The fur melted into his skin on most of his body, only his luxurious white collar remained and the tousled mop of red on his head with the pair of pointy ears sticking out of it.

He straddled my middle, his hands on my shoulders as I lay on my back under him.

"Oh, I missed you, Maxx." I cupped his face, gazing into those blue-and-green eyes of his.

"Cassy," he whispered softly, leaning down for a kiss.

"Cassidy!" The professor's voice sounded from the entrance into the corridor.

Maxx's lips had barely touched mine when he snapped back upright. Footsteps rushed down the corridor behind the professor.

"Don't move!" The largest Ivodian man I'd ever seen barged onto the balcony, shoving the professor aside. He was followed by the armed men from the atrium.

"Commander..." the professor started, but he was quickly lost in the tide of tall men in white uniforms flooding the balcony.

Maxx tensed. A low growl vibrated deep inside his chest. A flash of red sparked in his eyes all over again. He shifted down my thighs, standing on his knees. I sat up.

The men raised their weapons.

"Please..." I begged.

A laser fired with a flush and a hiss. Maxx's body jerked.

"No!" I cupped his face.

Deep longing burned in his eyes. And regret. He touched my cheek, wiping a tear I didn't know had escaped from my eye.

"Now, *I'm* the one who made you cry, Cassy," he said softly. "Of all the men in the world, I turned out to be the worst one for you."

"Maxx, no..." I threw my arms around him. "Don't say that."

The hissing sound of another shot came, followed by a thud of a dart embedding into his back. Someone tossed a rope. It snaked around his neck like a noose.

"Get it off him!" I yelled, shaking with rage and terror.

The men swarmed him, dragging him away from me. Leaving me all alone on the floor.

"Maxx!" I scrambled after them.

But the tide of armed men in uniforms had already receded, carrying my Maxx away with them.

"CASSIDY." THE PROFESSOR'S voice grated on my nerves.

I wished he didn't know my name. He'd been overusing it so much, the sound of it was making me sick.

"Please drink this." He shoved a glass of milky-white liquid into my hands.

He'd promised me Maxx wouldn't be immediately *decommissioned*, that he was safe for the time being. That was the only reason I was sitting here, in some small meeting room on the lower level, with Professor Xez. The only reason I was able to hear what this man was saying.

"It's for your own good," he repeated.

I stared at the glass without making any move to drink the liquid inside.

"I wish people would stop doing things for 'my own good' or for 'my own safety' and would just start being honest with me."

He heaved a sigh.

"Please drink it," he repeated. "Your body still needs help. You need nutrients and supplements after what you've been through."

"I didn't go through all of that alone. I would be dead if not for Maxx."

"I know—"

"He was with me, every step of the way. He suffered as much as I did. You found him passed out, just like you found me. He needs care and 'nutrients,' too. Why are you shooting at him instead of feeding him supplements?"

He placed a hand on my shoulder, and I shrugged it off.

"I'm not your enemy, Cassidy. The only reason Maxx still exists is because of *my* intervention." I glanced up at him, and he continued, "I submitted the report with my initial assessment of him, deeming him not immediately dangerous. In it, I requested to postpone the decommissioning order."

"Why?"

He sat in a chair across from me.

"I'm closely familiar with the technology used to produce those units. I've done a few scientific discoveries myself in the area. Their creation was remarkable. But Maxx's transformation is simply astonishing. He is proof that we now can give a machine the capabilities to grow and develop in a similar pattern as a real lifeform. He started out from a relatively small capsule of program code and genetic material. And now, look at him!"

"I wish I could *look* at him," I deadpanned. "But he isn't here, is he? Where are you holding him?"

The door to the room slid open at that moment. The giant Ivodian who had led the armed men in the attack on Maxx entered.

"The professor isn't holding anyone, Cassidy Davies," he said. "I am."

"You!" I jumped from my seat. Anger burst through me. The image of Maxx being dragged off by his neck burned in my mind.

"My name is Commander Ossux," he introduced himself but knew better than to offer me his hand. I would've refused it if he did. "This compound is under my command."

"Then use you authority for something good, Commander, and let Maxx go."

"I'm afraid I can't do that, Cassidy Davies."

As irritating as the professor's use of my name was, the commander managed to out-do him on that.

"Just Cassidy, please," I snapped.

The commander dragged another chair from the wall and placed it closer to ours, joining us in our "cozy" little circle in the middle of the room. He folded his massive body into the chair, making it squeak in protest, then placed his thick forearms on his knees and focused his dark-purple eyes on me.

"We will get you back to Earth at the first opportunity," he said. "Your family has already been notified of your whereabouts."

"Thank you," I said begrudgingly. "Can I call my parents?"

"Unfortunately, it's impossible to establish a communication link with Earth that would be stable enough for a video or audio call from here. You could write to them. But we may get you back to Earth shortly after the message arrives. Our spaceships are the fastest in the Galaxy," he said with visible pride.

My parents must have been losing their minds since the day I'd disappeared from the park. At least now they knew I was alive. Even as they probably still didn't have a clear idea how or why I'd been taken. I would most definitely write to them, but I couldn't leave here. Not on my own.

"I'm not leaving without Maxx," I said firmly.

"Maxx?" He squinted at me in question.

"Maybe you should learn a man's name, Commander, before dragging him on a rope to detain him."

He sat back with a smirk.

"I detained no man today, but recovered a lost machine, a malfunctioning piece of equipment. It has no name, just a number." He clearly meant every word he said. Maxx was nothing but an object to him.

Helplessness paralyzed my anger. I dropped my head into my hand, covering my face. This was what I had to fight against here—complete and utter ignorance.

"It is still a rather unique and expensive 'piece of equipment,'" the professor chimed in. "It would do well to treat him well."

"About that..." The commander rubbed his muscled thigh, as if searching for words. "Professor, you requested to keep it in commission for two more months."

Two months!

Was that all Maxx had to live?

"I'd like for you to reconsider your request. Please, withdraw it," the commander demanded.

"No." I glared at both.

"The unit proved dangerous," the commander insisted. "It has already injured three of my men. There may be casualties if it's kept at the compound for any length of time. It has to be neutralized. Immediately."

"Maxx isn't dangerous," I protested.

The commander glanced at me coolly.

"His behavior contradicts your words." He turned back to the professor. "My job is to protect this compound from the outside threat we're facing on a daily basis. I can't waste my time and resources on a threat deliberately kept *within* these walls."

"Then don't keep him here!" I exclaimed. "Let us leave. I'll take him back to Earth with me."

The commander scoffed. "The Earth's governments wouldn't want to have anything to do with this abomination the moment they learn all about it."

I feared the opposite. Some might be too eager to get their hands on Maxx, to use him for every sinister purpose he'd been created for.

"No one needs to know what he is," I argued. "He lived on Earth all of his life, without causing any trouble whatsoever."

"He's entered the final phase of his development," Professor Xez observed grimly. "His core programming has been activated. He is a soldier now, Cassidy. A walking breathing weapon."

Was the professor regretting his request to extend Maxx's life already?

I felt all alone in this fight. Desperation sent me out of my chair.

"*I* am Maxx's core programming." I pressed a fist to my chest. "*I* taught him everything he knows about relationships with others. It's because of *me* that he knows what it's like to care for someone or to have a friend. He knows the value of life. He wouldn't harm anyone if you…" I pointed my finger at the commander, "if you didn't attack him first. You treat him as a threat, leaving him no choice but to defend himself."

I pivoted on my heel to face the professor.

"And you aren't much better yourself, Professor Xez. Both of you made huge mistakes here. From the moment I found Maxx back on Earth, we've been inseparable. You found us on that ship together, in the same room. Maxx wouldn't leave me, even when the ship's AI tried to kill me. He kept me alive, risking his own life. And what did you do? You separated us. You locked him up without even talking to him. You didn't tell him where I was. And then you hurt him when he tried to get free. You tell me, the rational, intelligent men that I'm sure you think you are, how would *you* act were you in his place? Would you not defend yourselves and those you love? Would you not fight for your freedom?"

The commander cleared his throat and shifted in his chair, making it groan and squeak once again. The professor rose to his feet.

"May I have a word with you, Commander? I beg your pardon, Cassidy, but I think it might be better to clarify a few things between the commander and myself. Without the passion that leads you in this matter."

The passion he spoke about burned through me, making me tense and on edge. I was biased in this matter, I absolutely was. But I feared without me, their cold-heartedness would prevail.

I took a moment to reply, counting to ten in my mind to calm down somewhat.

"I'll leave. But only if you promise not to make the final decision without me." That was bold of me, to make demands of the two high officials on an alien planet I'd just gotten to. But there simply was too much at stake here for me to leave any of it to chance.

The commander got up.

"You will be informed." He approached the door of the room and slid it open. Folding his arms across his wide chest, he stood by the door, clearly indicating to me to get out.

Chapter 14

Cassy

Clutching a white plastic box with two sandwiches in my hands, I followed Professor Xez down the long gray corridor of the main building of the compound.

It had been ten days since I last saw Maxx. I couldn't recall us ever being separated for this long before, and it felt horrible.

Apparently, a lot of paperwork had to be exchanged between the military authorities and the scientific minds on Ivodi. Special arrangements had to be made in terms of my status on Rimall, too. But it'd been ten days, and Maxx was still alive. Even better, I was now allowed to see him on a daily basis as part of my new job, the Research Assistant on Professor Xez's team.

I'd put my college degree on hold for the time being, and the professor hired me based on my previous relationship with his research subject—Maxx. I was now officially employed on a two-month contract.

The professor brought me to the elevator, then took me down to the basement of the building. There were no windows here, just stone walls with metal doors in them.

"This looks like a dungeon," I said, following him down the narrow corridor underground.

"Um... Well. The security is the best here. The cells... I mean, the rooms are locked. Sometimes, when we encounter a new species of predator outside of the compound walls, we bring them here to study."

I scoffed. "So, Maxx is now treated as an animal. Is it a step up or down from being treated as a machine?"

With a soft huff, the professor let my snide remark slide, leaving my question unanswered. He stopped in front of a door on our left and opened it. We entered a small room with another door opposite from the first.

The room was brightly illuminated. A long desk with a panel of several screens stood on either side of the first door, with two men and the hologram images of three women sitting at each desk.

"Good afternoon, Professor," they all said, giving me curious glances. Humans were a rare sight on Rimall.

The top half of the next door was made of glass. The large room beyond it was painted white. A long gray couch stood by the wall. Maxx sat on one end of it. He stared straight ahead, but I didn't think he could see me. The glass in the door must be see-through only from my side.

He was dressed in the same white coveralls as everyone else in this building. Only the commander and his people wore different style uniforms, but those were also white. They didn't seem to have any other colors for their clothes around here.

Maxx appeared relaxed, his knees parted, his hands casually resting in his lap. But I sensed some hidden tension in him somehow.

"Does he know I'm coming?" I asked while one of the men at the desk verified my badge and my biometrics.

"He was told about your visit this morning," the professor assured me.

Maxx's expression remained unreadable. Was he expectant? Indifferent? Drugged out of his mind?

"Can we go in?" I shifted impatiently.

I didn't recall ever being this nervous in my life. My hands were so sweaty, I feared the box with sandwiches might slip from my fingers.

Professor Xez opened the door, and I followed him in.

"Good afternoon, Maxx," the professor said in an exaggeratedly cheerful tone of voice.

"Good afternoon, Professor," Maxx replied evenly.

Something about his manner was off. Strained? For once, he really sounded like a machine they all claimed he was.

"Hi, Maxx." I gave him a small wave with one hand, clutching the box to my chest with another.

"Hello, Cassy." The sound of my name made my chest tighten.

His ears twitched. They had always been the most expressive parts of his body. His ears and his tails. The tails lay motionless on the couch beside him, however.

He flicked his gaze from my face to the employee badge clipped to my belt, then glanced aside, saying nothing.

Did he see me working here as a betrayal? I only did it to gain access to him, to be closer, hoping I could do something, anything, in the few weeks he had left.

My throat tightened. My fingers gripped the stupid box. Had I really thought it'd be that easy to show up here with the sandwiches and pretend we were back home, as if nothing had happened? Had I expected Maxx to hug and kiss me and tell me how insanely grateful he was that I came down here for the first time in ten days?

I'd begged them to let me see him every single day, several times a day, but they wouldn't let me. Not until all the paperwork had been straightened out and I got this stupid badge.

Would it matter if I explained all of that to him? Somehow, I didn't think it would.

"Well..." The professor pressed a button on the wall and a large white screen slid down from the ceiling. "The controls are right here." He turned the screen on by pressing a button on the armrest next to Maxx. Previews of shows and movies appeared on it. "This is the list of the pre-approved programs. You can choose to watch anything you like. Enjoy the rest of your afternoon."

He exited the room, and the lock on the door clicked closed behind him. The glass in the doors and the walls proved to be one-sided, just as

I'd thought. From here, the doors and the walls looked white and solid. I wondered if Maxx even knew that he was being watched from the outside like a bug in a jar.

He remained in the sitting position on the couch. It was an impossibly long couch, almost twice as long as what I was used to. With him sitting on one end of it, there was plenty of space left. But I sat down next to him, with less than a foot of distance between us.

"I brought sandwiches." I opened the box and took one out, offering it to him. "It's the closest I could get to ham and cheese from what they have here. It smells almost like the real thing, though."

"Thanks." He took it from me.

Without even taking a bite, he put his hand with the sandwich back in his lap.

Awkward silence hung between us. I'd never felt so out of place next to him before. The uneasy feeling crushed me. I got the second sandwich out of the box and took a bite. It wasn't the same as back home. Nothing was the same.

"What do you want to watch?" I tipped my chin at the screen.

He shrugged. "Whatever."

I reached across his lap and pressed the button on his armrest. The first show on the pre-approved list began to play. It was Ivodian-made, and I couldn't even tell if it was a movie or a documentary. I had a hard time focusing.

Eating my sandwich, I didn't feel its taste. Instead of watching the screen, I took in the rest of the room. It was large, about the size of a school gymnasium, and appeared multifunctional.

Several machines or pieces of equipment were positioned around the room. I could only guess their purpose. A narrow bed stood in a corner, surrounded by screens. Was that where Maxx slept at night? Did they monitor him even in his sleep?

My attention returned to the man at my side. He'd taken a few bites of his sandwich and appeared to be watching the show, but I'd bet a kidney he didn't care about what was happening on the screen, either.

"Do you like the show?" I asked, desperate to break this unfamiliar awkwardness between us.

"What?" He tore his gaze from the screen, turning his head to me.

"Do you like it?"

He blinked, glancing at the sandwich in his hand, then back at the screen. If I had to guess, he hadn't even heard my first question and now was confused by what I meant by "it."

"You seem distracted," I said. "Is something bothering you? How have you been?"

He swept the room with his gaze, pausing on the machines, then the walls. His eyes then met mine straight on.

"Why are you here, Cassy?"

His question made the piece of my sandwich stick in my throat. Did he not want to see me? Would he rather I hadn't come?

I swallowed hard.

"I...I work here now." I fingered my badge. "So, I can come see you. They want me to hang out with you, like we used to do back home after school, remember?"

He nodded. His hand holding the sandwich flexed, forming a fist. The sandwich got squished, turning into crumbs and pieces of meat held together by the cheese paste.

"Will you come tomorrow?" he asked.

Did I hear hope in his voice? Or was it just wishful thinking?

"I will, Maxx. I'll come every day."

For as many days as they let him live.

Chapter 15

Cassy

A tap on my door made its screen light up. The smiling image of Professor Xez appeared on the screen.

"Are you ready, Cassidy?"

I nodded while placing the strips of cured meat over the slices of pink cheese arranged on the pieces of bread.

"Almost. Come on in."

The door slid open, and the professor entered my suite. The place wasn't big. It contained a sleeping space behind a white plastic screen, a small sitting area, a bathroom, and a food preparation counter with a sink.

I heard that long-term employees got much better accommodations outside of the main compound building. But I was here on a temporary basis and hadn't even been allowed to step out of the main building yet.

I finished making the sandwiches, scooped them up from the counter, and put them both into the plastic box.

"Does he like them?" the professor asked, tipping his chin at the box.

I sighed. "I'm not sure."

Everything about Maxx left me unsure lately. It'd been a week since we started spending an hour a day together each afternoon. Seven hours of awkward silence and brief, stilted conversations.

"What do you think?" I asked the professor. "How is he doing, in your opinion?"

He spread his hands aside. "Physically, he's in great shape. But as you know, we're forbidden to teach him about the full capabilities of his body and programming. The purpose of this project is for us to learn from him, not the other way around."

I nodded. That had been communicated to me at the very beginning. Maxx was not to reach his full potential as the weapon he was designed to be. The two-month extension had been given to the scientists for them to learn what parts of him could be used to improve the currently available technology for travel and space exploration.

As usual, the professor kept talking, "After Maxx fully recovered from your ordeal on the spaceship, his strength and agility have been growing and improving. So far, however, they're far from alarming levels."

"What will happen if they reach the 'alarming levels?'" I hated to ask, just as I hated to think about how alarmingly fast the first week of our two months had passed. But I needed to know.

The professor glanced over my shoulder at the window in my living area. Like everywhere else on this side of the building, I had a view of the wall draped in vines. It wasn't a hideous sight. The gray wall was almost completely hidden behind the green and purple vines with gorgeous pink and orange flowers in full bloom. But the wall was a constant reminder of the dangers lurking behind it.

"Please tell me there is hope for Maxx," I pleaded. "Even after you're done collecting as much data from him as possible in the next few weeks."

The professor crossed his arms over his chest and leaned against the nearest wall.

"The main goal of this project is to learn everything we can about Maxx. But I have a side goal as well. I've been monitoring his behavior to prove that he represents no danger to society. If he continues to act as agreeably as he has, I will file a request that he be allowed to live among people, with some necessary adjustments, of course."

That was great news. Only my mood didn't lift much.

"So, he seems okay to you?" I asked.

"Well, since the project officially began, he's been perfectly compliant. He's had absolutely no outbursts of hostility or aggression. Nothing."

Nothing.

That was the problem. Nothing I knew and loved about Maxx was there anymore. He didn't joke or smile. He hardly responded to anything at all. In fact, he acted very much like a machine, which drove me insane with worry. I couldn't sleep at night.

What if they were right? What if Maxx was nothing but a machine, after all? What if his entire personality was simply a series of codes and programs? What if the qualities I loved in him had been erased, and only the empty shell of the person I used to know remained?

The more I thought about it, the more the emptiness inside me grew. I'd been racking my brain, trying to figure out how to keep him alive. But what if the most important parts of him—his soul, his humor, his very personality—were already dead?

"Did you intervene in his...um, programming in any way?" I asked the professor. "His brains or software or whatever it is you would call it?"

The professor shook his head. "We only observe, monitor, and study, nothing else. We get the best results by watching him in his normal surroundings—"

I scoffed. "His surroundings are far from *normal*."

"They are as close to that as we could make it for him. He has a warm room with meals served to him regularly. He even has you to keep him company."

At those words, I felt like a failure. My company hadn't achieved anything. Did Maxx even care about my visits? He looked like he hardly noticed me at all.

"It can't be fun to sit in a windowless room all day," I said, thinking out loud. "Maybe I could take him for a walk outside? Just a walk in the outdoor gardens. Maxx used to like going to the park with me back when…" I let my voice trail off.

That time seemed so far away now. Maxx was so different back then, too. What did I even know about his likes and dislikes now?

The professor rubbed his chin in contemplation.

"We'd need to clear the gardens of all visitors for your walk. The commander wouldn't allow it otherwise, out of fear for people's safety. That is, if he allows Maxx to take a walk in the first place."

I might not know Maxx that well. But I knew Pumpkin. He used to love the outdoors. Running was one of his favorite activities of all times.

"He can't stay locked up for that long and be happy about it," I said. "He needs to move."

"Oh, but he has state-of-the-art exercise equipment available to him for physical stimulation of every muscle group." He glanced at the iridescent disk strapped to his upper arm. "We should go, Cassidy. It's time."

I grabbed the box with the sandwiches from the counter and followed the professor out of the suite.

"WHAT DO YOU WANT TO watch today?" I asked Maxx, leaning over his lap to reach the controls in the armrest.

"Whatever you want," he replied evenly.

Holding his sandwich in one hand, he lifted his arms up, giving me space.

I pressed the buttons, making the pictures on the screen shift. "Let's see if they have any shows from back home. Professor Xez said they got a few, just for us."

Propped on an elbow, I hovered over his thighs as he sat on the couch by the armrest. My side brushed lightly against his front, but our bodies didn't touch anywhere else.

"Oh, there is one!" I spotted a screenshot of a show I used to watch as a teenager. "Do you want to watch this one? I hope they have the entire season, not just this episode."

He remained silent, and I glanced over my shoulder at him. With both hands still up in the air, he was staring down at me instead of at the screen.

"Do you remember this show?" I asked.

"I do. I remember everything." His voice was soft, almost a whisper. And it held emotion—wistfulness so poignant, my breath caught in my throat.

My arm gave in, and I dropped into his lap.

"Sorry." I rolled onto my back and made a move to get up.

"Wait." He tossed his sandwich aside and placed his hand on my chest, just above my breasts.

My heart raced, and I wondered if he could feel it. I lay in his lap, staring up into his odd, multi-colored eyes. These weren't the eyes of a machine or an animal. They were Maxx's eyes, familiar and loved.

"This. Is. Torture," he said slowly, punctuating each word. "To have you here."

His words stabbed me like needles. My stomach hollowed.

"You don't like my visits?"

"It's not that." He shook his head quickly. "I *need* you. You keep me sane. Nothing about my life makes sense anymore, only you."

"Maxx..."

I covered his hand on my chest with mine. He freed it from me and moved it up to my neck, speaking softly but with quiet force behind his every word.

"Whenever they hook me up to a machine or hardwire me to a monitor, the thought of seeing you again is the only thing that helps me make it through the day. You are my one and only reason—"

A speaker clicked to life.

"Subject, release Assistant Cassidy Davies immediately," a stern male voice demanded.

Maxx's ears flattened against his head. His jaw flexed, and his eyes flashed red.

"He isn't holding me!" I sat up and shifted away from him, raising my hands in the air to demonstrate I was free to move.

I would've given anything to stay in his lap for just a little bit longer, but getting into a confrontation with authorities would work against us right now.

"Research Assistant Cassidy Davies, please rise and calmly proceed to the exit," the voice instructed.

Disappointment crushed me. "But I just got here. We have an hour."

"Due to a rule violation, this visit is now over."

"No, please..."

The couch suddenly moved, with me on it. Maxx had grabbed it by the armrest and hurled it across the room.

I squeaked in shock, drawing my legs up to my chest. The massive piece of furniture slid across the stone floor like a hockey puck on ice. It spun around about half-way through, then smashed with its back against the door.

Maxx leaped across the room and landed over me on the couch, one knee on each side of my hips.

"They have no idea, do they?" His voice came out strained and rumbling, as if he was holding back a roar.

There was nothing calm or impassive about his expression anymore. His lips pulled back, exposing the tips of his fangs. His eyes flashed every color they had ever been. Red, green, and blue alternated in them in some wild, insane pattern. It was both terrifying and mesmerizing.

Standing on his knees over me, he lifted me by my throat and one arm, making me slide up the back of the couch until my butt ended up sitting on top of it and my shoulder blades pressed against the wall.

"They have no idea what it's like to sit next to you for an entire hour and not be given a chance to touch you."

He kept one hand on my neck, keeping me in place without hurting. With the other, he punched through the control panel with the light switch by the door.

"Day after day, I've wished they would just kill the part of me that wants you. But that would mean they'd have to kill all of me. Because I need you with everything I've got."

He yanked a handful of parts and wires out of the broken control panel, then shoved his hand inside it. The lights flickered and died, plunging the room into complete darkness. The glow of his eyes was all that remained.

"Nine and a half minutes," he said. "That's how long it'll take them to realize that both main and auxiliary power sources are disabled and to find a way around that. That's all we have before they manage to open this door. Nine and a half minutes to spend one on one with you, in exchange for weeks of misery. A great bargain, don't you think?" He leaned against me, pinning me to the wall. "What should we do with such a treasure, Cassy? How do you want to spend the time we have?"

He sounded wild and possibly delirious. But alive. More alive than he'd been all the past week. I lifted my hands, touching his face, stroking his ears, raking my fingers through the fur on his neck.

"You're back..." I exhaled.

He leaned into my touch. "I've never left."

"I was so scared that you had. That I'd lost you somehow. That you no longer *knew* me."

He took my face between his hands. His thumbs skimmed my cheekbones. "They warned me that if I didn't stay calm, if I came too close, if I lost control, I'd never see you again. If I didn't do what they told me to do, they'd take the one bright moment in my life away from me. I couldn't let them have it. I did as they said. But it is a true torture to stay away from you."

"Don't stay away." I pressed myself closer to him. "Don't you ever stay away from me, Maxx."

He dipped his head, his mouth landing on mine in a kiss. The world twisted and spun, and somehow all of it, every single part of the Universe, fell back into place as he kissed me. All was right with the world once again.

I ran my hands along his wide shoulders, then moved them to his chest. I found the closure of his coverall in the middle of his neckline and slid it down past his waistline. Since he was wearing no belt, nothing stopped me from opening it all the way to his pelvis.

"Cassy..." he moaned against my lips when I splayed my hands on his bare chest.

His warm, masculine scent enveloped me. His hands skimmed gently up my arms. How could anyone ever think he was nothing but a killing machine? They didn't know him at all.

He opened my coverall. I unbuckled my belt, letting him take my clothes off me. He slid his hands over my body, not leaving an inch of my skin untouched.

"If only you knew how much I've missed you," he murmured, kissing my breasts. "I hate going to bed without having you at my side. Without you, my sleep is plagued by nightmares."

I ran my fingers through the wavy fur on his head. It caressed and tickled my skin, making me smile.

"I've hardly slept at all without you."

I had to find a way to change this. Now that we were together, everything seemed possible. I wasn't going to let them take him away from me again.

The soft caress of his tail slid up my leg. Another one traveled up my other leg. The tips of both stroked the insides of my thighs, then met at their apex. Air rushed out of my lungs as my body heated from the inside.

One arm pressed into the wall over my head, Maxx leaned closer. His other hand massaged my breast.

"I imagined touching you like this," he said huskily over my ear. "Kissing you... Making love to you. Every time I closed my eyes, I saw your face."

"Kiss me." I hooked my leg around his middle, drawing him closer as he took my mouth with his again.

The fur between his thighs tickled my skin. Then, I felt a different touch. One of his slick tentacle-like penises slipped between my legs, making me gasp in pleasure.

"I missed this sound," he murmured with a smile. "I love hearing your little gasps and moans. The best sounds in the world."

I moved my hips, searching for more contact. The tip of his prehensile length deftly swirled around my opening. The two others joined it, stroking along my folds and tickling my clit.

I wrapped my other leg around his waist, rubbing myself against him. Achy pressure throbbed between my legs, begging for a release.

"Maxx, I want you inside me..." I breathed out.

He tensed, and for a moment, I feared he would fight me on it. But he cupped my backside with his hand, shifting me up a little.

"I'll be gentle," he promised.

"I know you will."

This was definitely not the place where I'd imagined my first time would happen. Maybe, this wasn't the best time, either. But I had no doubt this was the man I wanted it to happen with.

Holding me with one hand, he cupped my chin with the other, lifting my face to his. The glow in his eyes softened before he kissed me.

One of his cocks continued to stroke me from the outside, while the other two swirled just inside my opening. I held on to his shoulders, moaning against his mouth as heat coursed through me, filling me with pure pleasure.

His caress remained steady and light even as my body heated, begging for more.

"Harder." I pressed myself to him.

But he kept it light, teasing, driving me mad with lust.

"More," I begged.

He moved a little faster, but still not hard enough. Pleasure skirted and ebbed. Pressure throbbed hotter, more urgent than ever.

"Please, Maxx..."

When I thought I couldn't take it any longer, he pressed harder, setting it off. Orgasm crested and burst through my body in fireworks of pleasure. It blended with the sting of pain as he thrust inside me. My hips rocked against him. I moaned from both pleasure and pain. The pain quickly receded, melting away in the last waves of my climax.

He shifted away, sliding out of me. I reached down, grabbing the tight rope of his cocks with my hand. He groaned against my neck as tremors of his orgasm rolled through his strong body.

The appetizing scent of baking spices drifted through the air. The tight spurts of his release hit the couch cushions below. Then he slackened against me for a moment of the most intimate closeness.

"I love you, Maxx." I nuzzled the side of his face. The confession came out so easily, so naturally. I'd always loved him, during all the years I knew him. Only now, the feeling was more real somehow, deeper—complete.

His chest moved with a deep breath. He lifted his head.

All I could see was just the faint bluish-green glow of his eyes, but I had a feeling he could see every single line of my face, even in the darkness. I looked straight at him. I had nothing to hide.

He stepped away from me and drew his coverall back up, fixing the closure in place. Then, he reached for my discarded clothes.

"Cassy, I'm thrilled you chose me to be your first," he said, helping me get dressed. "But I can't be your last. Or even your next."

"What are you talking about? You are my one and only."

His fingers trembled as he closed my bra, then held the coveralls for me to put my arms into its sleeves.

"They've connected me to their system enough times for me to learn the entire mystery of my creation and beyond. As they study me, I search their files. I finally know everything about myself. I also know that their plan is to kill me at the end of this project." I drew in a shuddering breath as he said that, and he placed his hands on my shoulders in a soothing gesture. "You know that, too, don't you?"

I knew, but I refused to believe that it would actually happen.

"I won't let them," I said firmly. "I'll find a way to stop them. There's still time to figure something out."

"I'm afraid there is no time anymore. Not after what I've done today." He buckled my belt for me and straightened the badge on it. "I broke their rules."

The light flickered on, flooding the room. I squinted and blinked. Maxx stared at me with his serene green-blue eyes.

"I'm sorry, Cassy, but my nine minutes are up."

Chapter 16

Cassy

"Get off the couch, Cassy." Maxx grabbed me around my waist, effortlessly lifting me from it as if I were a doll.

A humming noise came from behind the door, then a slamming crash. Any moment now, they would either unlock the door or break through it.

"Stay back." Maxx moved me away from him.

Rolling his shoulders back, he took a wide stance, facing the door.

He'd said they'd kill him. He knew that was what they would do once they got into this room. Then why was he standing there like that, waiting to be shot?

"Maxx." I moved closer.

"No, please." He held out a hand. "I don't want you to get hurt."

"Well, I don't want *you* to get hurt, either." I wrapped my arms around his middle, clinging to his side.

The humming behind the door grew louder. Something cracked.

"Cassy." He grabbed my arm as if to force me off him.

"Listen to me, please," I talked rapidly, running out of time. "You don't have to let them do it to you. You're stronger than them. Faster. You can fight this. They made you a weapon. So, be the weapon."

"You want me to kill?"

I wanted him to live. At all costs. I swept my gaze around the room, thinking fervently as the doors shook.

"You can run, Maxx. These walls are glass. You know that?"

He nodded, his brows moving closer in concentration. Of course he knew. He knew he'd been watched every second of every day. That was the reason he'd acted the way they wanted him to act even when there were just the two of us in this room.

"Behind the doors, there is another room," I kept talking, "a much smaller one, with another set of doors. They most likely will be open now, with all the commander's men barging in. Once you're out in the hallway, turn right. We're in the basement. There are no windows here. But the elevator is at the end of the hallway. You'll need this to operate it." I ripped the badge off my belt and shoved it at him.

He stared at the badge without taking it.

Another crack came from the doors, louder this time.

"Just break it!" Someone yelled from behind them.

"Take it!" I urged. "Once you're on any floor above the ground, there is no window you can't break, no wall you can't scale. Run! Be free."

He kept staring at me intently.

"What if I took *you* along with your badge?" he asked.

I glanced at the badge in my hand, then at him. It was an easy choice to make.

"Take me, then." I jumped into his arms.

I belonged with him, in every way. There was no one and nothing on this entire planet that meant more to me than this man.

He grabbed me with one arm around my middle, his hand under my ass, and I wrapped my legs around his waist. Holding his other arm in front of him, he leaped over the couch, smashing his elbow into the wall.

The glass wall shattered. The shards burst like in an explosion, flying in every direction.

I hid my face in the fur on his neck, peering out of it just enough to see the stunned faces of the commander and his men. Their mouths agape, they scrambled for their weapons. Maxx shoved them out of his way in a mad dash for the doors and out into the hallway.

He didn't pause, turning to the right and running so fast, we reached the elevator before any of the security men even made it into the hallway. I knew he was fast. But *this* fast? It made my head spin.

The doors of the elevator opened. Maxx grabbed the man who happened to be inside it and tossed him out.

"What floor?" Maxx asked when we were inside.

I slid my badge into the slot, and the elevator jerked up.

"It'll take us to my floor. That's the only clearance I have. It's seven floors above the ground."

He nodded. "Any windows?"

"Yes. One at each end of the corridor. The compound is surrounded by a wall as high as this building. There is also a metal mesh that covers the space above the compound like a ceiling, wall to wall."

The more I thought about it, the higher the doubt rose inside me. Was it even possible to escape the compound that was guarded and protected this much? Even for the super being that Maxx was?

"And Maxx..." I warned. "Don't forget about the wildlife beyond the wall."

He nodded again. The alarm blared when we reached my floor.

"Warning! A dangerous element escaped..."

I barely heard the announcement over the pounding of my heart.

The moment the elevator doors opened, Maxx ran for the window, jumped through it, smashing the glass, and...landed on the compound wall. Holding on to the top with one hand, he kept pressing me to him with the other.

"Can you try to move to my back?" he asked.

Doing my best not to look down to where the ground would be seven stories below us, I carefully eased one arm around his back, then shifted the rest of my body. With my arms around his shoulders and my legs around his middle, I clung to his back like a monkey to a tree. He wound a tail around each of my legs, like a rope to keep me tied to him.

"Hold tight," he instructed. "I need to use both of my hands to rip the net."

This thick metal net was designed to keep away the flying monsters that roamed the sky of this world. It needed much more than just bare hands to tear through. But his hands weren't exactly "bare," were they? Maxx's hands were tools on their own. His entire body was.

He shifted higher up the wall. Hooking an arm over the edge, he yanked at the net, easily tearing a hole in it.

"Hold on," he ordered, then climbed through the hole with me on his back. "You can move to the front again, now," he offered, hanging off the wall.

"Do I have to?" I whimpered, pressing my forehead to his shoulder from behind. Just the idea of letting go of him for even a second to shift positions made me dizzy. My stomach flipped at the mere thought of accidentally glancing down.

"No. You don't have to." He chuckled, petting my forearm. "You're good. Stay where you are, just keep holding on. I'll jump off the wall now."

Jump? Was he for real?

Holy cupcake. This was like jumping from the roof of a seven-story building. I shut my eyes tight, clamping my arms and legs so tightly around him, I surely blocked the circulation in both his body and mine.

And then, he jumped.

Chapter 17

Maxx

He spread his arms. They widened and flattened, stretching the short sleeves of his coveralls and catching the air to help him soar. Gliding over the tree canopies of the wilderness below, he looked for the best place to land. Cassy was right, the wildlife on Rimall presented a great danger. Everything and anything on this planet would want to eat them.

As if to prove that point, a winged shape descended from the sky and changed course to follow them. He sensed at least two more creatures right behind that one.

He scanned the forest below. It burst with life. His vision was so much better now than it had ever been before. Piercing through the layers of leaves, grass, and even dirt, he saw every movement and caught every shift in temperature.

Everywhere in the tree canopies and below, creatures big and small swarmed, hunted, and killed. They ate and were eaten. The only place with less activity was a cluster of bare rocks. Their gray peaks jutted out from the green, pink, and purple trees. He turned in the air, aiming for them.

As he got closer, he saw a stream rushing between the rocks. Further below, the water disappeared under the mountain, where he detected the cavity of a cave inside.

The winged creature above them squawked.

"Oh, God. What was that?" Cassy pressed herself tighter to his back.

He ducked into the tree canopies to lose their pursuant. It worked. The giant flying animal fell back, but it cost Maxx the distance. Instead of the rocks by the stream, he landed at the foothills.

The moment he set his feet on the ground, something lashed at his ankle. A tail or a tentacle with a spike on its end wound itself around his leg. He stomped on it, setting his foot free. But the spike pierced through his coverall and scratched his skin before slithering under a nearby bush and out of sight. The scratch burned with toxins, and he pushed the poison out of the wound.

Cassy relaxed her grip on him, but he immediately tightened his tails around her.

"No. Keep your feet up," he warned. "There are some nasty things on the ground. But you can shift forward. I want to see you."

Reaching behind him, he scooped her from his back and shifted her to his front.

"How are you?" He didn't need to ask. She was clearly terrified. Her eyes open wide, she looked around wildly.

"Something was chasing us, wasn't it? Up there? And what are the nasty things you mentioned?"

"It's all good now," he assured her, though there were certainly enough dangerous creatures around here to make them feel far from "good" if they weren't careful.

Cassy shifted in his arms, visibly on edge, despite his reassurances. "And you can fly! I didn't know that."

His arms had regained their regular shape the moment his feet had touched the ground. But the soaring sensation from gliding still echoed through his chest.

"Trust me, there are a lot of things you don't know about me." He grinned, happy to switch the subject from the dangers around them.

Faced with his smile, the tension on her lovely face eased. He loved how in tune their emotions were. It made it easy for him to calm her worries.

"I can't wait to learn all of your *things*," she teased.

He couldn't resist placing a kiss on the tip of her nose, which made her giggle. It felt amazing, not having to hold back any longer. He could kiss her as much and as often as she'd let him. And she seemed to love kissing just as much as he did.

She relaxed in his arms, resting her head on his shoulder. Only he couldn't allow himself to relax. The sounds of leaves rustling and twigs cracking came from every direction. The place was swarming with predators, looking to make a quick meal out of them.

"We have to get out of here," he said.

"Where do you want to go?"

"Up this mountain. There is a stream running down and into the rocks. Behind it is a cave. It appears empty. It should be a safe place to spend the night."

"You can see through the mountain?"

He nodded. "To a certain degree."

"Another useful skill," she muttered, shifting into a more comfortable position in his arms as he headed uphill.

He didn't argue with her, but this wasn't a *skill* that he'd honed, just a feature of his design that he'd discovered along with many others while in Professor Xez's "care." He even got to practice using it a little by scanning places obscured from his direct line of sight. Only back at the compound, he couldn't penetrate the walls of his room. Something stopped him, either in his settings or in the setup of the room. Either the professor or the commander—or both—wished to keep him in the dark about his location and surroundings.

Here in the open, the forest, the ground, and even the rocks were much easier to peer through. He could see the silhouettes of all the living creatures in the area and identify most of them. All of those he identified were venomous, vicious, or dangerous in some other way.

He had to get Cassy to a safer place. It was best not to stay in the open anyway, as the possibility of them being tracked or followed by the security of the compound also remained.

As he took the next step, something sharp pierced through the sole of his shoe and stung him between his toes. He sucked in a breath.

"What is it?" Cassy stirred. "Are you okay?"

"Yeah." He pushed the poison out of his skin and muscle tissue and made them knit together to seal the wound, all without slowing down or even skipping a step. "We're almost there."

He stopped on the rocks by the stream.

"Are we going to swim?" Cassy asked.

"I'll swim for both of us, but you'll have to hold your breath. Can you do that?"

She nodded.

A thick shape slithered down the trunk of a nearby tree behind Cassy. The creature's six long limbs moved quickly. Its mouth was already open. Its black tongue unfurled, studded with spikes.

He took her chin in his hand, not wanting her to accidentally turn around and see the monster getting ready to attack them. There was no need for her to get scared.

"Take a deep breath and hold it, Cassy."

The moment her chest expanded as she inhaled, he leaped from the rock and into the milky stream.

The water closed over them. Warm at first, it grew colder as he progressed underground. He had no difficulties holding his breath. But after a while, Cassy unwound her arms and legs around him. She shoved against his shoulders, kicking her feet.

She needed air. He wasn't fast enough in getting it to her, and she was trying to leave him to search for it.

He placed his hands on her waist and pushed her up to the surface.

She gasped and sputtered, breaking through.

"Wow..." she said after she'd caught her breath somewhat. "That was a long swim."

It wasn't that long. But time moved differently when one was fighting for their next breath.

He scanned the cave around the underground river. The milky water glowed softly with minerals dissolved in it. That was the only source of light in the cave. The semi-darkness didn't stop him from taking in every detail of the walls covered with long brown vines and the ceiling with the thick stalactites hanging from it.

Long, dark shapes slid through the water, circling Cassy and him. These creatures weren't venomous or big enough to seriously harm them, but it was best not to tempt fate.

"Let's get out of the river."

His arm around her, he swam to the riverbank and helped her climb up it. The rocks below the water were covered with shells. He broke one off on his way out of the river.

Cassy rubbed her arms. "It's chilly here."

"It's best not to start a fire, though." Coming behind her, he wrapped his arms around her and turned up his body temperature.

As he was warming her up, he kept assessing their situation, identifying the life forms around them. The white juice of the vines on the walls was pure poison. But each ropy length was enclosed in a thick layer of bark, making them harmless unless cut or chopped. The rocky floor was dripping with moisture. Other than the vines and the creatures in the water, there appeared to be no life in the cave. It really was the safest place in the forest. He exhaled with relief.

"Oooh, you're so warm," Cassy murmured, relaxing against him.

He shook his tails out. His high body temperature aided in water evaporation from his fur and their clothes.

"Do you want me to help you dry your hair?" He kissed the top of her head, next to her curly ponytail that looked a little disheveled after their flight through the trees and the swim underwater.

She touched her hair to assess its condition. "Nah. It's better to leave it as is. If I take the elastic out, it'll be a mess that I wouldn't be able to tame without my styling products. You know, I found some pretty decent substitutes for those here on Rimall."

She tucked the stray curls back under the elastic, and he stroked her ponytail with the tips of his fingers.

"I love your hair, Cassy. Always have. It's cute any way you wear it. Even as a total mess, as you call it."

"Aww. Who knew you'd turn into such a smooth talker?" She turned her face up to his. "Now I'm glad you didn't learn to speak earlier. If you did, you would've made me fall in love with you way before you were ready to love me back."

"I've always loved you, Cassy," he said sincerely. "In an ever-growing way."

She rose on her tiptoes and he kissed her. He didn't have a heart like she did. Several independent systems took care of that function inside his body. But a warm feeling throbbed deep inside his chest where a heart would have been if he had one.

She wrapped her arms around his neck, and he tightened his around her.

"It's so, so good to have you back, my pumpkin," she said with a smile. "I was so worried I might've lost you, that something inside you was erased forever. Like you remembered the words and actions, but completely forgot all the feelings."

"The feelings caused by you are impossible to forget. You never lost me. Never will."

"Promise?"

"For as long as I shall live," he vowed.

She kissed him again, then sniffed the air.

"What smells so good?"

A pleasant aroma wafted from the shell he kept clutching in his fist. With his body temperature elevated, the mollusk had been slowly poached in his hand.

"It's the shell I picked from the river. I didn't detect any toxins in it. But let me make sure."

He cracked the shell open and stuck the tip of his tongue inside it, running a quick chemical analysis on the mussel.

"Um...what are you doing?" Cassy asked.

He closed his mouth. "It's safe to eat."

"How do you know?"

"There are several hundred highly sensitive sensors in my tongue. It can detect the slightest amounts of harmful substances."

"Really?" She glanced aside. "And to think where that tongue has been."

He paused for a moment, then remembered the most delightful place his tongue had ever licked, and laughed. Grabbing her around her waist with one arm, he yanked her closer.

"Oh, it'll be there again. I can't wait to eat you out."

She released a soft gasp, followed by a giggle, the sound he loved so much.

"Listen, with all those super sensitive sensors... Did you perform an analysis while you were going down on me?"

He'd laugh again if she didn't seem genuinely concerned, biting her full bottom lip.

"Sweetheart," he murmured, nuzzling the side of her face. "When I'm with you, most of my functions shut down. All my focus is on you and the pleasure your body gives me. I have nothing left to do any real analysis."

"Not much different from any man then, are you?" she teased. "Mom always says men have just one thing on their brain."

"Mhm..." He kissed her.

Just like that, his focus started to melt. The taste of her took over his senses. From her mouth, his thoughts jumped to all her other delectable places to kiss, to lick, to suck, and nibble on.

The shell slipped from his fingers and rolled onto the stone floor of the cave.

"Oops," Cassy laughed.

"See? You stole all my concentration. I even forgot to feed you first."

"It's not your job to feed me."

"It's not a job at all. I just want to take care of you. The best I can, considering the circumstances."

She had taken care of him for years. It thrilled him to do the same for her now, on a slightly different level, of course.

He got more shells from the water as Cassy sat on the riverbank. Then he warmed them up between his palms, steaming them gently, two or three at a time.

"There is some salt in their meat, but sadly, I can't get any real seasoning around here right now," he said apologetically. He wished to give her the world but couldn't even offer her a bottle of hot sauce with her dinner.

"No worries." She sat on the rock, folding her legs under her and eating the mussels he gave her. "These smell like pickles and don't taste bad at all."

He ate some too. The biological parts of his body needed the nourishment obtained through eating. Though, he could go without food for a very long time if needed.

He wondered if Cassy was thinking about that as well, since she seemed to study him as she ate. She watched him dive for the mussels, then stared at his hands closely as he steamed the shells between his palms.

"Fascinating," she finally said.

"You like what you see, baby?" He flexed a bicep and winked at her in a super cheesy way.

She burst out with laughter at his antics, then slapped his arm lightly. "It's a good thing you already have me. Because that act would never get you laid otherwise, buddy."

He grinned, happy he made her laugh.

"But in all seriousness," she said. "The things you can do are mind-blowing. And I'm sure I've only seen a small portion of them."

"The list of the functions is huge," he agreed. "And when you take into account all combinations of them, it's practically endless. Besides, I also have the ability to learn new things. So..."

This wasn't him bragging. He had just stated a fact. Frankly, he'd give up all these amazing functions in exchange for an average body of a regular guy that would allow him to continue living a quiet life with Cassy somewhere safe.

"They really went all out with creating you as a super soldier," she said. "The Ivodian way of life largely depends on the exploration of other worlds, I've learned. They have a vast fleet of giant spaceships with each crew numbering in the hundreds. The men spend years on those ships, traveling to distant planets. They mostly explore and scout for resources now. But decades ago, there were still some wars going on, too."

"Right." He tossed an empty mollusk shell back into the river. "There is not much use for me now."

Hurt and bitterness stirred in him once again at the thought of the decommission order he'd found in one of the security files in the professor's folder. The commander was much more careful with the documentation. He always kept sensitive info in a section of the system that Maxx couldn't access. But the professor let that one slip out, allowing Maxx to find out what the future held for him. As it stood right now, there was no future for him at all. Ivodians saw no use in him, just threat.

"But that's not true," Cassy protested. "Look where they live." She moved her arm in a sweeping gesture around the cave. "I wouldn't have lasted a minute out here on my own. You know how clumsy I am sometimes. Without you, I would've stepped on something or eaten something, or petted something that would've killed me."

"You don't have to be clumsy to die here, Cassy. I've been stung twice on our way here. Had I not gotten rid of the poison, I would've died too."

"You got stung. Where?" She looked alarmed.

"In the leg, then my foot. But I'm fine. I swear," he assured her. "I pushed the poison out and healed the wounds right away."

"You can do that?"

He grinned. "Yep. One of those amazing functions from my list."

She stared at him in wonder for a moment, then lifted a pointer finger up.

"See? That's what I mean. You didn't die. You got rid of the poison. You flew away from those pterodactyl-birds that chased us. You figured out what to eat for dinner. You are surviving just fine here, and you've kept me alive all this time, too. You were made to survive in these conditions better than anyone else in the entire Universe."

"I actually have parts of some of the local animal species. I was made here, remember? They used local resources."

It still made him feel uneasy to think about himself as being "made," rather than "born" like everyone else in the Universe. But the concept was slowly settling down in his brain. Cassy's acceptance had a lot to do with that, he suspected. Her opinion mattered to him the most.

"That's exactly what I'm talking about," she said passionately. "You are amazing."

"Thanks," he deadpanned.

She slapped his arm again. "Stop it. You know what I mean. Even if you weren't the love of my life, even if I was a complete stranger, I'd still see the benefit of having you around. Especially on a planet like this."

"Did you just say I'm the love of your life?" He knew exactly what she'd said. He'd recorded every word of that sentence to playback for the rest of his life, no matter how short that life may end up being. But happiness tingled warmly inside him, and he just wished to hear her say she loved him once again.

She rolled her eyes, but the smile on her face remained warm and as sweet as ever.

"That's what I said, Maxx. I love you. There isn't anyone out there who could ever take the title of the love of my life away from you. But you're missing my point. The commander and the rest of them should be ecstatic to have you on their compound, instead of trying to get rid of you."

"I represent a threat. That's what scares them."

"People are often afraid of the unknown. But they've had a chance to study you. They know exactly what you are."

"And that scares them even more." He got up and went to rinse his hands in the river.

Cassy sat on the rock, staring straight ahead of her. Her brow furrowed in a frown, she chewed on her lip nervously.

He hated to see her worried, but he could do nothing to assuage her concerns. Tomorrow would be another tough day to survive. That was all he could give her—day-by-day survival.

Despite sensing no immediate threat in the cave, he decided it was best to stay off the ground for the night. For that, he peeled several vines off the wall and wove them together into a hammock of sorts.

"That's neat." Cassy tested its strength by placing her hands on it and leaning into it with her upper body.

"It'll hold us both," he assured her, having already calculated the strength of his construction. "The juice inside the vines is toxic, but the bark is thick. You'd need an axe or a saw to cut through it."

"Or your claws," she quipped, climbing into the makeshift hammock.

She was right. His fingernails extended into sharp blades that could slice the vine in half.

He smiled, joining her in the hammock. "I'll keep the sharp edges hidden."

She snuggled against him, sliding her knee between his thighs and splaying a hand on his chest. He pressed his face into her hair, breathing in her scent.

For the first time in days, he slept without nightmares. He dreamed he was finally home again.

Chapter 18

Maxx

Cassy's cold, nimble fingers slipped past the closure of his coveralls. A shiver ran through her body as she pressed herself to him.

"Cold?" he asked, rubbing the sleep out of his eyes. He could be alert and ready for any action instantaneously if needed. But he kept alerts to a minimum. The slow, lazy way of waking up in the morning felt more natural and far more enjoyable, especially with Cassy cuddling up against him.

"Mhm..." she dug her hands into the fur on his chest.

He hugged her tighter and raised his body temperature a little. "Better?"

"Mhm." She shoved her feet between his calves. The socks she was wearing clearly didn't do a good enough job at keeping her feet warm.

A few minutes later, however, she seemed to relax a little, warming up. He thought she might have drifted to sleep again, but her fingers moved. Raking them through his fur, she stroked his chest. The tip of one brushed his nipple, sending a zap of desire through his body. He sucked in a sharp breath.

"You know what's weird?" Cassy kept circling his nipple, driving him insane with desire without even realizing what she was doing. "They designed you without a bellybutton, which makes sense. But then they went ahead and gave you nipples, which are useless for men of any species."

His mouth felt dry as he breathed faster, fully awake now. He had to clear his throat before speaking, "Mine aren't useless."

"Really?" She tilted her head back, turning her face to him. "What are they for? Can you shoot lasers out of them or something?"

He chuckled. Lust, not lasers, shot through his body from the sensors in his chest, one of which Cassy was stimulating with her finger ever so innocently. His cocks strained, taut like metal rods. A little longer, and he'd come right then and there.

"They are a part of the same system as my cocks," he explained in a strangled voice.

"Oh..." Her eyelids fluttered, and she moved her hand to the center of his chest, leaving his nipple alone. "I can't feel your heart." A shadow of concern moved over her face.

"Sorry. I forgot. Let me fix it." He shifted the setting gauge inside his ribcage, back and forth, back and forth, syncing it with her heart. The action produced a soft thudding noise, similar to a heartbeat, the only one he could have. "There you go."

Surprise replaced the worry on her face, her eyebrows rising toward her hairline. "Can you start and stop your heart at will?"

"No... It's not like that." He hesitated, feeling foolish about his little ruse.

This was one case when he didn't enjoy talking about his differences with Cassy. Because at least in this one thing, he wished he could be just like her. He wished he had a heart. However, he didn't want to lie to her, either.

"I don't have a heart, Cassy," he confessed.

"You don't?" The confusion on her face grew even deeper. "But how do you even function without one? And what is this?" She pressed on his chest over the shifting, thudding gauge.

"I have other systems that perform the function of the heart. Three of them, actually. But they operate too smoothly, without any beating. This here is..." He shifted his gaze aside before confessing, "It's a mechanical gauge that makes a soft thud when the settings are changed. So... I just shift it back and forth."

"Why?"

"To produce the sound similar to a heartbeat."

She tilted her head, staring at him intently. "Wait a minute. So, you keep adjusting a part you don't need to adjust because it helps you produce a sound similar to a heartbeat?"

"Right. Ever since you were a kid, you liked placing your hand right here." He put his hand over hers on his chest and shifted them both a little to the left. "Just like that. You always fall asleep with your hand here, even now."

A smile stretched her lips. "Yes, I do."

"It calms you, I know, and helps you fall asleep."

"So you created a heartbeat, just for me?"

He loved the way she said it.

"Just for you," he echoed.

She leaned in for a kiss, and he took her mouth with his. His hand slid from his chest to hers. He cupped her breast through her coveralls. She moaned as his thumb stroked over her hardening nipple. A zap of energy rushed through him in response. His cocks jerked harder than ever.

"I want you, Cassy," he murmured against her lips. He always wanted her. What delighted him was that she seemed to crave him just as much, too.

She opened his coveralls all the way down, and he promptly slid hers off her shoulders, then unbuckled her belt.

The scent of her skin was both familiar and exciting. She scraped her fingers over the ridges of his abs, and his hips jerked, his cocks springing rod-hard from the fur between his legs.

"You like belly rubs, don't you?" she giggled.

He winked, melting inside from pleasure. "Rub me anywhere you want, sweetie." He flipped her over on her back and tugged her bra cup down, freeing her breast. Circling the dusky tip with his fingers, he watched her eyelids flutter closed in pleasure. "Does my touch do to you what yours does to me?"

She released a soft moan, arching her back. He slid his hand into her underwear and cupped his hand between her legs.

"How are you feeling this morning?" he asked.

He wished for nothing more than to take her again, but he held back, conscious of her first time being just last night.

Her eyes snapped open. "*I'm feeling* like you owe me a lot of sex, pumpkin, after making sure I didn't get any before you."

Well, if sex was what she wanted... He slipped a finger inside her, curling it against her inner walls. A groan of satisfaction fell from her lips.

He worked her with his hand until her moans grew louder and she rocked against him faster and faster.

"Oh...I need you, Maxx."

She reached for his cocks, and they snapped tightly around her fingers the moment she touched them. His pleasure spiked at the contact.

"Come closer." She tossed her leg over his hip, bringing their lower bodies flush against each other.

Removing his hand from her, he stroked and caressed her most intimate spot with his prehensile cocks. The three of them spread around, rubbing the tight bud of her clit, teasing inside her opening, and stroking along the sensitive skin of her inner thighs.

She gripped his arms as her climax rocked her body. Her mouth fell open, with sweet, tiny whimpers coming from her lips. And he couldn't hold it back anymore.

Winding his cocks tightly together, he thrust all three of them into her. Hot and slick, she welcomed him, wrapping her legs around him.

"Oh, God, you're hot..." she hissed.

"Sorry." His body had overheated, lust coursing through him in a wild torrent.

He lowered his temperature, barely in control of his systems. After a few frantic thrusts, he jerked his hips away from her, coming on the rocks under their hammock.

Pleasure rippled through him, as he clung to her. She smoothed the fur on his head, stroking the back of his ears. The unhinged storm of pleasure finally calmed down to a warm, languid current of bliss. He shifted off her, then slid under, drawing her onto his chest.

"Who knew sex could be this great?" She played with the long fur on his chest. "Though, I have a feeling it's only this wonderful because it's with you."

He couldn't stop staring at her. Her flushed lips and sparkling eyes presented a gorgeous picture to behold. She was everything and everywhere, in every cell of his body.

She glanced at the rocks below the hammock. "You said you've learned a lot about your body now. Do you know what that is?" She pointed at the glistening puddle of his release. "Is it really harmful for me?"

"No. It's not toxic or anything. But it's best for you to stay away from it."

"Why? I'm on birth control, remember?"

He heaved a long breath. "I was meant to reproduce aggressively, to spread the genetic material stored in me in order to create superspecies. My offspring wouldn't be cyborgs. They'd have no metal or electronic components, but they'd be faster, stronger, and physically superior to any sentient beings out there. Once the genetic material is in a female body, it doesn't deteriorate. It'll wait for as long as it takes for fertilization to occur."

"Wow. Your swimmers are persistent little buggers, aren't they?"

He snorted a laugh. She sure had a way of putting it.

"Right. And by the way, it doesn't matter what way they'd get inside your body."

"What do you mean?"

He tugged at a springy curl that had made its way out of her hair elastic. "Swallowing them won't kill them."

"Oh... Good to know." She bit her lip, thinking about something. "Is that why it smells so appetizing? To entice women to swallow it?"

"Possibly." He hadn't seen any mention about his scent in the documentation he'd studied about himself. But if the point was to get his genetic material into a woman's body by all means necessary, making its scent appetizing made sense.

She sighed. "It's too bad. I like pumpkin spice."

"Is that what it smells like to you?"

She smiled. "Pretty close."

She filled his vision entirely. He wished to focus all his senses on her and only her, but a warning alarm pinched his insides.

Something was wrong.

A splashing noise came from the underground river, then a slap. A gray-blue tentacle rose from behind Cassy. It ended with a wide, round flipper, tipped with claws.

She didn't see it, still smiling at him. And he hated to alarm her, knowing she'd be scared. She'd been afraid so much lately.

"Close your eyes, sweetheart," he said, gently shifting her from him.

"Why?" She shook her head, but thankfully did as he said.

"Just keep them closed for me, please?"

"What are you going to—"

The tentacle lashed their way, and he grabbed it. Jumping off the hammock, he yanked at the appendage in his hand. A giant head appeared from the water, the size of a small car. The monster's mouth was wide open. Several rows of teeth rotated inside it like some grinding machine from a nightmare.

A strangled gasp of horror behind him told him that Cassy had opened her eyes, after all.

"I've got it," he assured her without taking his attention off the slimy creature crawling up the riverbank.

The tentacle in his hand tensed. He flexed his muscles, straining to keep it trapped. Another undulating appendage rose from the water. Then another one. How many did this thing have? He'd run out of hands to hold them all.

The creature jerked its tentacle, pulling him toward its mouth with grinding teeth.

"Oh no, you won't," he gritted out, clenching his jaw.

Extending his claws, he sliced through the tentacle, cutting it off. The shapeless body of the monster convulsed. It released a loud gurgling sound. Clear liquid gushed from the stump.

Maxx slashed at the next tentacle with his claws that were long and sharp like blades. The second tentacle dropped to the ground, cut in two. It was promptly followed by the third.

Gurgling and splashing in the opaque water of the underground river, the monster finally retreated.

Maxx chased it into the water and raked his claws along the creature's long, wiggly tail, lest it entertain any ideas of returning to bother them again.

He waited at the water's edge until the dark-gray mass of the monster had completely disappeared into the water and every trace was gone.

"Are you okay?" He rushed to Cassy, who was hiding behind their hammock.

"Yeah..." She let him hug her. "Are *you?*"

She touched his chest and arms, then grabbed his hand and inspected it closely.

"I'm good."

He'd hidden his claws, and the river had washed off the gore and slime from his fingers.

"Good, good..." she kept repeating, as if trying to convince herself.

Her heart was still beating wildly in her chest. Her eyes remained wide open in horror. Despite his best efforts, she had been scared. Terrified. She just tried to hide it, taking big, deep breaths.

"It's gone now?" she asked.

He longed to reassure her, to tell her no monster would ever scare her, not even in nightmares. But how could he promise her that? This planet was a real nightmare. Creatures like that water beast were swarming it, on the ground and below it. He couldn't promise Cassy with any certainty that the water creature wouldn't return or that some new monster wouldn't attack them before the day was over.

"It's gone," he said. "For now."

Drawing in a shuddering breath, she nodded. She understood.

"I'll have to be more vigilant—" he started, but she cut him off by squeezing his fingers.

"You have been doing an excellent job at protecting me, Maxx. But this can't be your entire life. You can't keep fighting wild beasts without a moment to relax."

"That's what I was made for." He shrugged.

"Maybe. But you're so much more now than what you were designed to be."

Her faith in him and her acceptance thrilled him. For Cassy, he wanted to be the best man he could be. He wanted to give her everything. But she was right. With the two of them being out here on their own, the best he could ever give her would be hardship and survival.

"Do you want to go back? To the compound?"

She shook her head quickly. "Not if they'd kill you on sight."

"Then, I'll have to make sure they don't see me. At least not right away." He grinned, hoping his smile would reflect on her face, too, the way it'd often done before.

"What do you mean?"

"We'll sneak in. Quietly."

"Are you sure that's what we should do? Go back?"

He nodded. "Cassy, you can't live the rest of your life in a cave and be happy. Away from civilization, your friends, and your family."

Her sensual mouth formed a firm line of determination.

"Oh yes, I can. And I would if that meant you'd stay alive. But I've been thinking." She worried her bottom lip between her teeth. "I wonder if we could still come up with some agreement with the rest of them."

"What kind of agreement?"

"I'm not sure exactly. Something that would allow you to exist and for us to be together."

He wrapped his arms around her, bringing her closer. He didn't believe the Ivodians would ever allow them to be together. But she deserved much, much better than wasting away in this cave with him.

She stroked his chest, sending a new shiver of pleasure through his system.

"I don't think we've tried everything yet, Maxx. I keep thinking I could've done more... That I should've been more convincing."

Would that have made any difference? He didn't think so.

Yet he asked. "You want to speak to the commander?"

"Oh no." She exhaled a brief humorless laugh. "That man is hopeless. He's so stubborn and unapproachable. But the professor may be able to help."

"Professor Xez?" The memories of all the invasive procedures that man and his team had put him through made his skin crawl.

"Yes," she spoke enthusiastically. "I can talk to him. He knows you better than anyone in that place now. He also holds a pretty high position on Ivodi. He must be able to do something."

Professor Xez had been in charge of this project ever since they had landed on Rimall. But the professor had done nothing all this time. Maxx didn't hold much hope about things changing in the past twenty-four hours since they'd left. But if Cassy wished to speak with the man...

"If that's what you want, then that's what we'll do," he agreed. "We'll go back."

She added quickly, "Only if it doesn't end up costing your life."

That was a guarantee he couldn't give her.

Chapter 19

Cassy

"Wait. They've fixed it." Holding me with one arm to his side, Maxx crouched by the net attached to the top of the wall around the compound.

The tear he'd made in the mesh when they'd escaped had been mended with a patch of new netting. The metal of the patch was shiny. However, the seam that attached it to the main net was rough and uneven. The repairs had been done hastily. The emphasis had been clearly on the functionality, not aesthetics.

Maxx tore at the net, making a new hole in it, large enough for us to fit through.

I held on to him tightly, but unlike the last time we were up here, I wasn't scared. I trusted him not to drop me. His strong arm around my middle, combined with the tight hold of his tails on my legs, gave me all the reassurance I needed.

"You make it look like it's a cheesecloth," I said. "Not a metal net meant to withhold attacks of vicious predators."

"It's because I might be the most vicious of them all."

"Yeah? Well, my vicious, if anyone does so much as point a weapon at you, I want you to grab their stupid heads and stick them where the sun doesn't shine."

He laughed. "You know, Cassy, I can literally do exactly what you just asked for. It'll be messy. And it won't look pretty. But I can do it, I can stick their heads up their asses."

I made a face, not doubting he could.

"I guess I have to be careful what I wish for around you, since you're so adamant about making all my wishes come true. Let's just hope it won't come down to *that*. Let's talk to them first, okay?"

He didn't look very hopeful, and it broke my heart to think he might be right. But I had to try.

"Ready?" he asked when we were on the other side of the net.

I tightened my arms and legs around him, clinging to his front.

"I am."

He let go of the wall and...soared. He spread his arms out like wings, and they took the shape of wings. They flattened and thinned, becoming wider and giving us lift.

I wasn't sure how far he could really fly, but gliding seemed easy to do for him, even with me attached to his chest like a baby sloth.

"Steer around the main building." I cranked my neck, to see some of the compound below us.

Last time, I'd had no chance to take a good look at it. The sight was beautiful from this height.

The main building was the highest one. Behind it was a cluster of lower ones, painted in cheerful yellow. These housed the hospital facility and the staff quarters. The entire complex was surrounded by luscious gardens.

Draped in vines with flowers, the massive walls of the compound didn't feel as imposing in this part. They stood back, opening up to a place that looked like a small, quaint town with trees, garden paths, and flower beds bursting with flowers of every shape and color.

"It's nice here." I couldn't help but admire the view. "As it should be, since it's a hospital. People from the Rimall's moons come here to get treatment and recover."

"Is it the first time you're seeing this part?"

"Yes. I wasn't allowed to leave the main building."

With my temporary permission to stay on Rimall, my clearance was limited, allowing me to move in and around the main building only. Since I was officially employed by the professor, I also was allowed to visit the highly secured wing where Maxx had been held.

"Where to, now?" He asked, circling the building with the hospital's lab and offices.

"That large round window on the corner, right there." I pointed. "With the purple flowers on the ledge. It must be the professor's work room. He said he'd asked for the purple flowers to be planted under his window. They remind him of his home on Ivodi."

Making a wide turn in the air, Maxx descended to the ledge under the window and landed among the flowers.

I climbed off him and peered through the window with my hands cupped on each side of my face. The spacious room seemed empty. There was no one at the many workstations arranged throughout the room. The small sitting area with low chairs and tables was also unoccupied.

"He isn't here," I said, feeling deflated with disappointment.

"Maybe he went to grab lunch or something? And will be back soon?" Maxx was clearly trying to cheer me up.

To my knowledge, Professor Xez usually spent the first half of the day right here, in his workroom at the hospital. Later in the afternoon, he'd be normally escorting me to see Maxx. But right now, it was too early even for lunch.

"We can wait until he comes back," Maxx said.

Waiting on the ledge was unwise. Someone could see us standing here.

"We should at least get inside." I inspected the window frame. "I've no idea how to open this—"

Maxx tapped with his elbow against the glass. Just once. Lightly. And the glass shattered.

"Like this?" He grinned at me.

"Well, I guess..." I climbed through the broken window into the room. The thought of how easy it'd been to break for him wouldn't leave my mind. "Is it hard to hold back your strength?"

He shrugged, following me in. "It's just a matter of figuring out what level of power to operate at in each situation. I have different settings."

I stepped over the pile of glass on the floor under the window. The shards were so small, some appeared almost pulverized.

"I fear you might've used the wrong *setting* in this case," I muttered under my breath.

He gave the glass an unconcerned glance. "I might have."

A muffled sound of a fan turning on came from behind the door to the left. In one fluid movement, Maxx stepped between me and the door, shielding me from it. His ears twitched, following every imperceptible-to-me sound, then lowered to his head as the door opened. Professor Xez walked in, adjusting the closure of his coveralls. Sighting us, he froze with his hand halfway up the front of his torso. By the look of it, there must be a bathroom behind that door.

"Cassidy." The professor said my name, but his cautious stare snapped to Maxx.

"He won't hurt you," I said quickly.

My words did nothing for the professor's unease, it seemed. He moved his gaze to the broken window, then back to Maxx.

"We just want to talk," I assured him.

"Can we have a minute of your time, please?" Maxx said calmly. "One-on-one and preferably without you raising an alarm, if possible."

The professor cautiously lowered himself onto the stool at the nearest workstation.

"Do you promise not to hurt me?" he asked.

Maxx strolled over to the station and picked up a shiny, cylindrical object from the long, narrow desk.

"You mean the way you hurt *me?*"

He pressed on something and a cluster of long, sharp needles sprung out from the cylinder, each of them pointing in a different direction. I gasped, staring at the sadistic-looking tool.

"What the hell is this? Did you..." I glared at the professor. "Did you use this thing on Maxx?"

The man shifted on the stool uncomfortably.

"I... We didn't know to what degree he's capable of feeling pain. I'm sorry if some of the earlier tests might've been...um, unpleasant."

My stomach knotted, making me nauseated.

"Unpleasant?" I scoffed. "What the fuck, Professor! You never told me about that type of *tests*."

He stirred awkwardly under my glare. "I'm sorry. I really am. As soon as we realized our mistake, we immediately corrected it. We switched to less intrusive instruments and equipment. They made it longer to obtain accurate results, but..." He flicked his gaze back and forth between Maxx and me. "What is it about? This visit? Do you want revenge? An apology?"

Maxx winced with disgust, tossing the offensive tool into the bin under the table. I stepped closer to him and placed a hand on his arm.

"I had no idea..." No wonder he'd acted so guarded and withdrawn with me during my visits. How could he trust me if I worked for his tormentor?

"I know." He patted my hand, then moved his attention back to the professor. "I have no use for your apology. That's not why I'm here. I'm more interested in talking about the future, not the past."

The professor cocked his head. "What about the future?"

"I wish to have one." Maxx leaned with his hip against the table. "I want to live for much longer than a few weeks."

Professor Xez cleared his throat. "Well... um, the decommission order for the end of the project has been removed. Now, you're supposed to be shot on sight."

"What?" I gripped Maxx's arm tighter.

"Of course." He didn't seem that surprised.

The professor rubbed the back of his neck. "Unfortunately, after your escape, Commander Ossux declared you a confirmed threat to the compound and removed me from the decision-making process on this matter. My project was canceled that very day. I've been given two weeks to wrap up my lab work here at the hospital and leave Rimall." He lifted his eyes to Maxx. "I'm sorry, Maxx, but I have absolutely no authority in your case anymore. I'm afraid there is nothing I can do."

Chapter 20

Cassy

The disappointment was crushing. Our situation had turned from bad to terrible. Maxx was no longer a research subject. Now, he was considered one of the biggest threats to the compound. He was hunted.

To be shot on sight.

I rubbed the chill of dread out of my upper arms. "We can't stay here, then."

A shadow crossed the window, plunging the room into semi-darkness. I whipped around to find a giant...*something* landing on the window ledge outside. It was the color of yellow mustard. Long like a snake. With what looked like hundreds of clawed feet on each side of its body.

Knocking flowerpots off the ledge, the creature stuck its long beak through the broken window and opened it, displaying its tongue that looked like a serrated blade. A loud, repulsive sound—similar to the one people make when they vomit—ripped from its throat.

I blinked, covering my ears with my hands. "What is *this?*"

Alarms blared before anyone could answer me.

"Attention. Attention. Perimeter breach. Please take cover, lock the doors, and stay away from the windows," the announcement came from the speakers under the ceiling.

The professor jumped to his feet, sending his stool crashing to the floor. The yellow beast was slithering into the room already. Its long body spilled through the window, coil after fat, glossy coil fitted with claws.

"Stay back." Maxx stepped between us and the creature. "Professor, take Cassy to the bathroom and lock the door. Stay there until it's safe—"

The mustard-colored monster lashed with its tail, not letting him finish the sentence. A tassel of long, curved spikes on its tail rattled menacingly, with bright yellow liquid dripping from their ends.

Maxx ducked, leaping aside.

"Go, Cassy!"

"Come." The professor urgently tugged me by my arm.

But I couldn't move. The giant snake-centipede snapped its beak at Maxx. It tossed a coil of its body over him, trapping him in the thick, undulating loop.

He gritted his teeth. His shoulders tensed, veins bulging in his temples. His face elongated. His jaw widened, the fangs descending. His body grew, pushing the coils of the monster aside. His coveralls were torn, and pieces fell to the floor. With a deafening roar, he shifted into his beast form.

Sinking his teeth into the yellow flesh that trapped him, he tore a chunk out of it. The creature quacked loudly from pain. Its coils loosened, but not for long. Snapping its beak and clicking its tongue, it readied its claws for an attack.

The door to the room slid open with a swish.

"Stand back!"

Commander Ossux rushed into the room, dressed in his full battle uniform, complete with a black helmet and a chest plate. He was followed by his similarly outfitted security men. In addition to the sleek white laser guns, they carried nets, chains, and other equipment that looked more like traps and snares than weapons.

"All civilians, clear the area," the commander ordered, his focus snapping to the two beasts entangled in a battle by the window. He then waved his arm at his men. "Shoot to kill. Both."

Both?

"No!" I screamed.

The commander frowned my way. With the spark of recognition in his purple eyes, his expression turned tired.

"You."

He acted as if I'd made his life so much more difficult ever since appearing at his perfectly secured compound. Except that it hadn't been my choice to be abducted and dragged here all the way from Earth.

"Please, don't shoot Maxx," I begged, pressing my hands to my chest.

The commander's frown deepened as he moved his heavy glare from me to the professor.

"Which one of you controls him?" he asked.

"No one," I scoffed. "Maxx is perfectly in control of himself."

"Well, in that case, leave the room and let my unit handle this." He motioned toward the snarling beasts tangled by the window.

The commander's men moved closer, shouldering us out of the way. One of them steered the professor toward the exit. I swerved, evading the hands of the Ivodians who tried to stop me, and rushed to the commander. He raised his weapon.

"Leave Maxx alone!" I shoved at his arms, making him lose his aim. "He isn't an animal or some wild beast for you to shoot."

With feral roars, Maxx ripped through the flesh of the snake-monster. Its dark red blood sprayed the room's white walls.

The scene didn't exactly support my claims, but I insisted, "Maxx is an intelligent being, capable of feeling, learning, and understanding."

The commander exhaled an exasperated breath, glaring at me. "Why are you even here?"

"To give Maxx a chance!" I screamed over the noise and growls of the fight. "You can't kill him in cold blood. All he wants is to be allowed to exist." My voice shook. Tears choked me.

The snake-monster slapped the heavy coils of its body against the floor. The commander moved back a shoulder, as if shrugging me off, then lifted his laser gun once again.

Panic rose to my throat. It would take less than a second for him to pull the trigger. When I needed a few minutes to plead our case and be heard.

"Please..."

Maxx leaped up, the loops of the snake dropped from him. He landed on all fours in front of the commander. Maxx pulled back his lips, baring his long teeth sharp as daggers.

He was so much stronger and faster than any of these men. They had no idea what exactly they were up against. He could scatter them around like a bunch of tin soldiers. He could slit their throats open before they even realized what was happening to them.

But he just stood there, his three tails swaying in warning behind him. Then, the outline of his body changed. His features shifted into the face of a man again. He stood upright, staring straight into the barrel of the commander's weapon. A man, no longer a beast.

"I have no weapons." Maxx lifted his hands, palms turned to the commander. His hands were weapons on their own. But the sight of his bare palms enforced his message. "I'm not going to fight you. Shoot if you must."

"No..." I whimpered, clutching my hands in front of me so hard my nails dug into my skin.

The commander paused. And I was afraid to move, afraid to breathe, trying to read his thoughts in his stern weathered features.

He was trained to kill wild predators to protect people's lives. But he wasn't facing a wild beast right now. He stared down the barrel of his gun at the face of a naked, unarmed man who spoke calmly and wasn't attacking anyone. A man who'd just fought a dangerous creature, protecting the compound. The man who had fought on the same side as the commander did.

I hoped that was what Commander Ossux was thinking about. I prayed he saw Maxx for what he truly could be—an ally.

The snake-monster raised its head behind Maxx and opened its beak with a hiss. Its tongue unfurled, like a flexible saw blade.

Commander Ossux jerked his weapon up. With a bright flash, the laser ray zoomed over Maxx's shoulder and seared the beast's tongue. The snake recoiled to the window and lashed its tail.

The long spikes separated from the end of its tail. Hurled across the room, they flew at the commander.

Jumping high, Maxx twirled in the air, graceful like a dancer. His tails swished, giving him lift and direction. He stretched, catching the spikes in his arm and shoulder. The yellow liquid trickled down his skin and fur, leaving black, charred grooves in both.

He landed on his feet, but his knees gave in as his face distorted in pain.

"Maxx!" I ran toward him.

Several slim Ivodian tails slapped around my arms, legs, and waist, stopping me from reaching him.

"The poison will kill you on contact," the commander warned, holding me tightly in the snare of his seven tails.

He ripped off his breastplate. A few drops of the yellow liquid had burned groves in the hard metal and indestructible plastic of his armor. Some of it worked its way through the entire plate as he held it in his hand, his arm outstretched to keep it away from us.

"But how about Maxx?" I yanked at the restraints of the commander's tails. But he trapped me tight.

With Maxx out of the way, the commander's men opened fire on the snake monster, chasing it back out of the window. Bleeding and weak, the creature had lost most of its viciousness. It climbed over the windowsill, its claws slipping and tripping on its way out.

"End it," the commander ordered, and his men ran out of the room in pursuit of the predator outside.

Maxx lay on the floor, propped up on his left elbow. At least a dozen long black spikes were sticking out from his right arm and shoulder. The poison was eating through his flesh.

"Maxx, you can push it out, can't you?" I spoke through tears. "You've been stung by nasty things before."

"It's way too much poison for him to deal with." The professor moved closer, away from the door.

Maxx reached for a spike with his hand.

"Don't touch it." The warning in the commander's voice stopped him.

Anguish racked me at the sight of Maxx lying there alone. His face paled. The fingers of his injured hand trembled. He may be a super being, but he was clearly in pain. There were enough people in the room, but no one came to him.

"Can someone help him? Please!" I yelled, pulling frantically against the commander's tails holding me prisoner.

"May I?" Professor Xez made his way around us.

He had a pair of flexible metal gloves on and carried a rectangular container in one hand. He carefully stepped around the sprinkle of drops of poison on the floor next to Maxx. It had already burned little holes through the plastic mat and left black pockmarks in the hard material underneath.

My heart fluttered with hope. "Can you do something?"

The professor kneeled by Maxx's side. "I'll try."

From the box, he produced a cylinder with a nozzle, then sprayed a bluish liquid on Maxx's arm and shoulder. As it connected with the poison of the spikes, the liquid foamed.

"Is it the antidote?" I asked anxiously.

"Something like it. It neutralizes the poison, preventing further damage." He sprayed the chemical on the pocked floor, too.

"Please don't waste it," I groaned.

The professor raised a brow ridge at me. "But we don't want the poison to eat through the floor to the level below."

"We don't want it to eat through my Maxx!" I yelled, my patience dangling on a very tiny thread.

"I have enough to treat him too," the professor assured me calmly.

From under the nearest workstation, he dragged a bucket filled with pieces of smooth white cloth. He sprayed the blue liquid on the cloth, then grabbed one of the spikes embedded in Maxx's arm with it.

"This will hurt," he warned.

"I figured," Maxx gritted through his teeth. His voice was strangled; he clearly struggled to breathe, but he remained awake and alert.

He held still, only wincing a little and releasing a small throaty sound when Professor Xez yanked the spike out of his flesh. Bright yellow poison dripped from the spike's end. The professor caught it with the white cloth that promptly turned black as it soaked in the poison. He then placed the spike into the rectangular box where he'd had the spray cylinder before.

"Would you pass me that bin over there, please?" He asked the commander.

The commander shoved the bin from under another table closer to the professor. He stared at the black cloth that the professor tossed in the bin, then at the spike in the box.

"This much poison would kill my entire unit." The commander's eyes focused on the mangled arm of poor Maxx.

"Maxx is tougher than all of you," I said to the commander, keeping my eyes glued to the professor's hands as he pulled another spike out of Maxx. "Very few things can harm him." I turned to face the commander, meeting his glare straight on. "He'd be a great asset to have on any team, but especially on a planet like Rimall."

The commander's eyes narrowed.

"Where did you spend the night?" he asked.

"In a cave in the forest. Have you ever spent a night outside of the compound, Commander? Alone? With nothing but the clothes on your back?"

He stretched his neck side to side but didn't reply.

I continued, "How about being stranded out there with a human woman in tow? Someone who needs constant protection from all the monsters in that wild jungle? Could you keep her safe until the morning? Without a single scratch on her helpless, defenseless body?" I gestured at myself the best I could with one of his tails wound tightly around my wrist.

Maxx stirred, a faint smile stretching his paled lips. "You weren't that helpless, Cassy. You did great."

Despite the situation, a warm glow spread through my chest at his words. "You're just being nice because you like me, Maxx. I know I was a handful."

Professor Xez pulled another spike out and tossed it into the box. "Did you like having Cassidy in the jungle with you, Maxx?"

The question seemed casual and even random. But from what I knew about the professor by now, he must've asked it for a reason.

Maxx gazed at me. One green eye, one blue. Both shone with so much warmth and tenderness, even the veil of pain couldn't hide that.

"I'd have her everywhere with me," he said. "Anywhere she's willing to follow me."

The professor studied the face of his former subject for a long second.

"Maxx cares about me," I explained. "With all his heart."

The professor looked doubtful. "He doesn't have a heart. These units weren't designed with one. There are three systems—"

I interrupted him by stomping my foot, since my arms were effectively tied by the commander's tails.

"Stop dissecting him, Professor. For once, look at him as a person not a study subject. A man can have a heart without possessing the actual organ, just like some people with living beating hearts in their chests can be utterly heartless. Maxx has a heart so huge, he made a heartbeat, just for me. He cares about me. Why is that so hard to accept?"

The professor seemed to consider my words while pulling more spikes out of Maxx.

But the commander scoffed. "Caring is not part of this unit's programming."

I clenched my teeth, forcing myself to count to ten before I said something I might regret.

Not taking his eyes from his work, the professor observed quietly, "We found his core programming severely compromised, Commander."

I remembered Maxx saying something about the AI on the "haunted" ship complaining about the same thing, too.

"It's true, the units of that series were programmed as brutal killing machines," the professor continued. "But they were designed with an AI component. AI stands for artificial *intelligence*. Their creators couldn't possibly predict every complex, dangerous situation in which their super soldiers might find themselves in the future. As a result, they had to make them able to 'think' for themselves, to learn new things, to evaluate problems, and to come up with solutions on their own."

Maxx was capable of all of that and more. His actions and logic didn't differ from that of any other person. To me, he *was* a person.

"So whereas the core programing remained the same," the professor kept talking, "it needed to be reinforced during the unit's consequent development stages. Installing it wasn't enough, it had to be taught as well."

"Kind of like raising a child?" I asked.

The professor tilted his head. "Right. So, as Maxx's nature remained that of a ruthless, cold-blooded killing machine, his upbringing failed to reinforce that for him. Instead, something else had a profound effect on his development." He met my eyes. "His friendship with you became the most defining factor in his learning. Instead of developing his tactical abilities, calculating battle strategies, and finding the most effective ways to kill, Maxx ended up learning how to care for another being. He was exposed to human culture and its core values. He was raised in a family unit, instead of a lab. All of that had its consequences."

Delightful consequences, in my opinion, if it resulted in the man Maxx had become. My gaze crossed with Maxx's, and my chest filled with love and pride for him.

The professor finished pulling out the spikes and sprayed more blue liquid over Maxx's mangled flesh on his arm and shoulder.

"Can I come closer?" I pleaded.

The professor nodded. "Just don't touch the affected area yet." He put a clean white cloth on Maxx's wounds and the cloth charred black quickly. "The poison is still there."

I tugged impatiently at the coils of the commander's tails looped around me. He finally loosened his hold on me. I shook his tails off me and rushed to Maxx.

"Hey." I sat on the floor and placed his head in my lap.

"Oooh, that's nice." He exhaled slowly, then closed his eyes with a smile.

I raked my fingers through the fur on his head and neck. I kissed the pointy end of his ear, and he moved it, gently stroking it against my lips.

"Since Maxx is no different than any other person now," I said, mostly addressing the commander, since everything depended on him at this point. "He could live the rest of his life like one, couldn't he?"

The commander's jaw flexed. His mouth flattened into a hard line. "We have a combat unit that doesn't obey its core programming. It could mean he is not just dangerous but unpredictable."

"Aren't all of us unpredictable to some degree?" I asked. "Can you guarantee any person's behavior one hundred percent at all times?"

"No. But I don't run the same risk with a *person*. If one of my men gets stung by an *elears* plant, for example, and runs wild with the *elears* madness, chances are we'd stop and treat him before he causes too much damage. A cyborg, on the other hand, would raze this compound to the ground and kill every one of us inside."

"No he won't. Unless the *elears'* toxins are as corrosive as this one," I pointed at Max's wounds, "he'd just push the poison out of his body, heal the sting site, and go on with his day. You wouldn't even know he'd been stung. "

The commander looked at the professor for confirmation.

"That would be the more likely outcome of that case scenario for Maxx." The professor nodded, applying a clean dressing on Maxx's wounds. This time the cloth didn't change its color. The poison had finally been fully neutralized. "How do you feel?" he asked Maxx.

"Fine." Maxx moved his shoulder with a slight wince.

"Can he have a painkiller, please?" I asked.

"A painkiller?" The professor blinked. "Do you really need one?"

"Of course he does," I said before Maxx managed to reply. "It hurts. Why would you let him suffer if you can lessen the pain? Please give him something."

"All right." The professor shrugged, getting up.

Picking up his damaged breast plate, the commander inspected the holes burned through it. I watched him carefully, my heart beating with hope.

"He saved your life today," I said.

"While I had my gun pointed at him." He cast a glance at Maxx.

"Exactly. What other proof do you need that his priorities are in order?"

He rubbed his chin, saying nothing. Maxx watched him carefully. Even his chest went still as his breathing halted.

"Give me a chance, Commander," he said quietly. "I promise you won't regret it."

The professor returned with a syringe.

"An analgesic," he explained before injecting the medicine into Maxx's arm.

Maxx didn't even flinch as the needle sank into his flesh. His attention remained on the man who held his fate in his hands.

"What would you do if you had a whole life ahead of you?" Commander Ossux asked.

A smile played in the corners of Maxx's mouth.

"I'd live it. Just like anyone else. I'd spend my life with the woman I love. Raise a family with her. Have a job. Make friends. And enjoy the sunshine." His smile disappeared as he met the commander's eyes straight on. "I'll always protect those I love, but believe me, I find no joy in violence."

The professor put the empty syringe aside. "I've already sent my report to Ivodi. But I will add my analysis of today's incident to it."

The commander shifted his weight to another foot. His tails undulated wildly behind him, making me wonder how they didn't knit into knots with all that activity.

"I'll write my assessment too," he finally said to Maxx. "I'll also send a recommendation to allow you to join my team. Clearly, your ability can be useful around here." I sucked in air, afraid to believe things might be looking up for us. He lifted a finger with emphasis. "On a *probationary* basis. For the first three months, your behavior will be closely supervised and evaluated daily."

Maxx smiled broadly. "Thank you, Commander. Like I said, you won't regret it."

Relief flooded my veins with warm tingles as the tension drained from my body and soul.

Maxx will live.

"Thank you," I exhaled. "Thank you so much."

I hugged Maxx's head, covering his smiling face with kisses.

The commander grunted at our gratitude, rolling back onto his heels.

"The decision on your immigration status will have to be made by the proper authorities on Ivodi," he warned. "But I will submit all the necessary paperwork." He slid out a disk from a holder on his sleeve. "As a person, you'd need proper identification. Should I submit *Maxx* as your given name?"

Maxx nodded.

The commander entered notes into his disk. "How about your family name?"

"Davies," I said quickly. "He grew up in my family. It should be his last name all along."

The commander glanced up from his disk. "Do you wish to be listed as officially related?"

"No." I blanched. Maxx and I grew up together, but it certainly didn't feel like we were siblings or any other kind of blood relatives. "We're not really related."

"Not yet," Maxx said, flashing me a grin. "But we will be. If Cassy agrees to it."

My cheeks warmed up. Was he proposing to me? Here? Now?

"Am I the woman you love?" I asked, remembering what he'd just told the commander about his plans for the future. "The one you want to have a family with?"

He lifted his hand and gently cupped my face.

"There's no other, Cassy. Never was. Never will be."

Chapter 21

Cassy

"How are you feeling?" I asked, leading Maxx down the hall toward my suite in the main building of the compound.

"Excellent." He grinned. He hadn't stopped grinning ever since...well, ever since he got the second chance at life.

"Are you sure?" I eyed his right arm and shoulder. Both looked like one giant wound, his flesh charred and disfigured. The professor had slathered lots of healing gel over it. It solidified into a flexible clear dressing, temporarily replacing the damaged skin.

"Positive." Maxx lifted his right arm and moved it around. "See? It's healing already."

I shook my head, not that convinced. "It must be just the painkillers working."

"That too," he agreed, kissing the tip of my nose. "Thank you for those, by the way."

"I can't believe the professor didn't think about giving them to you himself."

He shrugged. "The pain wasn't that bad."

I had a hard time believing it.

"You were lying on the floor, Maxx."

His grin turned cheeky. "Yes, but you kept rubbing behind my ears. It felt so good, I didn't want to get up."

I stopped in front of the door to my suite and gave him a look. "Is there anything you wouldn't do for a belly rub or for scratching behind your ears?"

He laughed. "I'd do anything, as long as you're the one doing the rubbing and the scratching."

I shook my head but couldn't help smiling as I let him in through the door.

"The suite is small," I said, somewhat apologetically. "It was meant to be temporary."

Before we'd left the hospital building, the professor had mentioned that if Maxx and I were approved for a long-term residency, we could move into one of those quaint staff homes on the other side of the compound.

Maxx gave the place a quick look.

"It's perfect," he said, wrapping his arms around me and drawing me closer. "I don't care where I am, as long as I'm with you."

"Me too, Maxx." I closed my eyes and buried my face in his chest. I couldn't believe he was with me again. And this time, he was here to stay.

I hugged him, vowing in my heart to never let him go.

Three months later.

"TIME TO GET UP, SLEEPYHEAD." A kiss landed on my cheek, followed by one on my nose, then another one on my bare shoulder. "It's moving day, remember?"

Oh, right. We were moving today. Maxx had passed his probationary period without a single complaint or disciplinary action against him. All the official papers were done. His job became permanent, and he and I were approved to move into a much bigger place in the employee section of the compound.

I also was able to transfer my studies to a college on Ivodi, which I could now complete remotely, combined with the practice in the hospital on Rimall. They needed nurses here more than anywhere else. And I was promised a permanent position, too. Which was convenient, since the focus of my studies had also been switched to Ivodian medicine, not human.

Maxx placed another kiss straight on my lips. "Breakfast is ready."

I drew in a long breath. The air was filled with appetizing aromas of coffee and fresh pastries.

"You baked? Again?" I stretched, opening my eyes.

The face of the man of my dreams appeared right in front of me. I knew he was real, but it still felt like a dream to have him here with me every morning.

"You keep feeding me," I murmured, pulling him closer for another kiss.

He obliged, kissing me gently.

"You've fed me for years. It's my turn now." He nuzzled the side of my neck.

I giggled as his fur tickled my chin. "I fed you kibbles and stinky dog treats. And you've been making gourmet meals for me every day. It's not the same, pumpkin."

He laughed at the nickname before kissing my neck. His hands were propped on the pillow on each side of my head. But his tails... His tails were everywhere.

One slinked under the covers, caressing my bare legs. The other one lifted my sleeping shirt, dragging it up past my chest. And the third one stroked my exposed skin from my knee, up my belly, then around my breasts.

The long, silky fur of his tails caressed my skin like the lightest feathers. Warm tingles of pleasure rushed through my body, warming my blood.

He swirled the tip of his tail over my breasts, making my nipples pebble. The tip of his other tail slipped between my thighs. The gentle caress of the fur against the sensitive skin of my inner thighs made me whimper with pleasure.

"Coffee?" He lifted his head, making a move to get out of bed.

"Don't you dare." I hooked a leg around his hips, keeping him exactly where I needed him—over me. "You're not leaving, not even for a second. Coffee can wait."

A flush of heat in his eyes told me that was the option he preferred too. He got me out of my nightshirt, and I unbuckled his pants. He wasn't wearing a shirt, which made things easier. I ran my hands over the hard squares of his abs and combed my fingers through the long, silky fur on his neck and chest.

He freed his legs from his pants and kicked off the soft shoes he wore, then climbed over me.

"Coffee can wait," he echoed in a raspy voice, then lowered his head, dragging his tongue over my hardened nipple.

I gripped his head, my blood running faster through my veins. One of his tails was working me between my thighs, and I opened my legs wider in invitation. His cocks moved against my skin, all three hard and eager.

"Take me, Maxx," I moaned impatiently.

He growled against my breast. With an arm around my middle, he flipped me over. I lifted my ass for him, wiggling it eagerly.

"Come here." He gripped my hips and yanked me to him. With his hand between my shoulder blades, he pressed my upper body into the mattress.

I turned my head to the side, my breasts squished against the soft surface. Anticipation was buzzing through me. Need pulsed with an ache between my thighs.

"Please, Maxx..." I begged, and he slipped a finger inside me.

"Is this where you want me?" he asked wickedly, swirling his finger to stroke my inner walls.

"Yes..." I exhaled.

"How about here?" He slipped his finger out and dragged it up from my front to my back. He circled my back opening.

"Oh… I…" We haven't done that yet. But I wanted to try it.

A slight tendril of trepidation added to my excitement.

Maxx leaned over my back, kissing the shell of my ear. "Where do you want me, sweetheart?"

"Everywhere," I breathed out. "I want you everywhere."

He nibbled on my ear. "So be it."

One of his cocks slid smoothly inside me. I moaned from its slick glide against my inner walls. Another one gently prodded between my butt cheeks. I tensed, and he made the third one curl against my clit.

"Tell me if you want to stop." He rubbed gently. Pressure throbbed more intensely between my legs, begging for a release.

"Oh no, don't stop. Please…" I rocked my hips against him, matching his rhythm.

Lost in the warm wave of pleasure rolling over me, I hardly noticed his intrusion from the rear. But the sensation of being impossibly full felt invigorating. Two of his cocks were inside me, yet separated, driving me crazy with pleasure. The third one remained outside, stroking and rubbing against my clit.

"Oh, God…" I panted. "Why have we never done this before?"

"Because I feared you'd blow all my circuits like this," he groaned. "Like you're about to do now… Cassy, you feel so damn good."

He yanked me to him, sinking deeper inside me. My breasts dragged along the top sheet, teasing my nipples. I gripped the blankets as he pounded hard into me.

Leaning over my back, he covered my hands with his, and I laced our fingers together, keeping him in that position.

"Cassy, sweetie," he pleaded. "I need to pull out. I'll come…"

"Stay." I flexed my fingers, keeping him in place.

He was made to reproduce at all costs. The only way to avoid that was to keep his genetic material out of my body. But I no longer wished to avoid him or keep him out of anything.

"I'm on birth control," I said, stroking his hands with my thumbs. "Until I get off it, your stuff will be just sitting inside me, right?"

He kissed my shoulder. "But what if birth control fails?"

"Then it fails. And we'll have a baby."

He paused. "Is that what you want? To have a baby with me?"

"Oh, Maxx..." It might be awkward timing and position to have this conversation, but it felt too good to change. I wanted all his cocks exactly where they were, caressing all my pleasure spots inside and out. "I want to have everything with you. I love you. Always have."

"I love you, too, Cassy," he said softly, moving inside me faster again. "Only you."

Pleasure burned higher. I gasped as orgasm rocked through me with blissful spasms.

With a strangled roar, Maxx jerked on top of me. His hands shifted. Long claws sprung from his fingers, piercing through the sheet and into the mattress. He roared louder, pumping his hips into me. My insides felt warmer. The sensation spread through my lower body, tingling and throbbing. With hardly any time in between, a second orgasm exploded through me, even more intense than the first.

I moaned wildly through the swells of pleasure rocking me. Maxx's body relaxed on top of mine for a moment, then he hugged me around my waist and rolled us to the side.

"Did you shift?" I asked as we both were catching our breath.

He pressed his lips to my shoulder, holding me tight, my back to his chest.

"I... I don't remember."

I took his hand, catching the glimpse of his claws the moment before they disappeared completely.

"Looks like you did. At least partially. And you don't remember it?" I turned in his arms to face him.

A huge, satisfied smile spread across his lips. "It was so fucking good, Cassy, I might've passed out for a moment. All I remember was pure pleasure and...you."

He kissed my hair that now was out of my ponytail and all over my head, thanks to him.

A shadow of worry crossed his handsome face. "Did I scare you?"

"No." I shook my head with a smile. "It was actually more hot than scary. Maybe..." I twirled a finger in the fur on his chest. "Maybe you could do it again one day?"

He arched an eyebrow. "You want me to shift?"

"Would it be something *you* want?" I asked tentatively.

His eyes glinted with excitement and promise. "Well, if my beast form doesn't scare you..."

I placed a kiss on his lips. "None of your forms scare me, Maxx. I love them all. Every. Single. One. Of them." I punctuated my words with more kisses.

He laughed happily.

"Come here, you." He gathered me in his arms.

I relaxed, my body molding so perfectly into his.

He buried his face in my hair.

"Next to you is my home, Cassy. The only home I've ever known."

Epilogue

Cassy

Next year, October 31st.

"Are you okay? Do you need any help?" I fussed around Maxx as he piled our luggage onto two carts at the spaceport.

"I'm fine. Promise." He chuckled, easily pushing both carts through the crowd on the way to the hall where the interplanetary travelers were greeted by their loved ones.

I might have packed a bit too many suitcases, I had to admit as I watched them all teeter precariously on top of each other now. But it wasn't every day we traveled to visit Earth. This was our first trip home since Maxx and I were abducted by the rogue AI.

I brought presents for everyone—samples of non-perishable Ivodian food for my friends and family to try, clothes, fashion jewelry, and souvenirs, or "trinkets" like Maxx called them.

"Cass, baby!" My mom separated from the crowd of people waiting in the hall and ran to me.

Tears sprung to my eyes as she threw her arms around me. It'd been almost a year since I'd last hugged my mom. We'd exchanged messages regularly and even had a couple of video calls when Maxx and I had visited Ivodi. But it felt so incredibly good to finally get to hug her again.

"Mom!" I pressed her to me. "I missed you. So, so much."

She smelled like home, and my childhood, and everything wonderful and never-forgotten. Tears glistened in her eyes when she leaned back.

"Oh, it's so good to see you." She sniffled. "How have you been? How was the trip?" She cupped my face, kissing both my cheeks.

I had no chance to reply.

"Cass." Dad made his way to us through the crowd. He tore me from my mother's arms and wrapped me into a bear hug of his own. "So good to have you home. How have you been?"

His dark eyes glistened with tears, too, making my throat itch with emotion. I forced a smile, lest we all start bawling right here in the middle of the spaceport.

"I'm good," I said, cheerfully. "We both are good." I gestured at Maxx, who stood nearby, guarding the luggage carts. Wearing a trench coat, a pair of dark pants, and a scarf, he looked rather smart and elegant.

Both my parents turned to him.

"Hi Maxx." My mom hugged him.

He beamed at her. "It's so nice to see you again, Mrs. Davies."

"Oh, just Trisha, please. We're a family, always have been. And now, you guys are making it official next week."

Next Saturday, I was going to marry this man, in front of our closest friends and family. We had waited with the wedding ceremony because we wished to have it here, on Earth, surrounded by the people we loved. Mom was right. This was Maxx's family as much as it was mine.

"Hello, Maxx." Dad hugged my soon-to-be-husband, too. He then tilted his head, taking in Maxx's impressive height from his feet to the peaks of his ears. "Boy, you've grown." He slapped Maxx's arm lightly, making him laugh.

"Since you last saw him, he's grown a couple of times, actually," I chimed in.

Mom rubbed my arm. "It's so, so good to see you both. Well..." She glanced around. "Let's go home."

The crowd was moving all around us, people bumping into us and our luggage.

Dad gave the two piles of our suitcases a concerned look. "We'll need to get a van for a taxi."

"Or a highway truck," Maxx deadpanned, making my dad chuckle. They both grabbed a cart each and moved toward the exit, leading the way for Mom and me.

"Hey!" Someone yelled from the crowd. "Nice costume!"

Maxx's ears jerked toward the sound.

"Thanks."

His tails moved, peeking out the back slit of his coat.

I noticed quite a few people in costumes in the crowd. Some were dressed up as aliens since we were in a spaceport, after all. Some might have been real aliens, too.

"It's Halloween today, isn't it?" I remembered today's date.

This was the one day of the year when Maxx fit right in. On any other day, I suspected, we would've gotten far more stares and questions. Aliens of any planet were still a very rare sight on Earth. Even here in the spaceport, the crowd was predominantly humans who traveled to the Moon for vacation or visited one of the attractions orbiting the Earth.

Of course, being the only one of his kind, Maxx would stand out on any planet in the Universe, not just on Earth. He surely realized that, but it didn't seem to bother him. He walked confidently toward the taxi parking area, his tails swaying, his ears up.

My mom hooked her arm through mine, pulling me closer.

"I just don't know how I will be able to let you leave ever again," she groaned.

I smiled. "Mom, we just got here, and you're already worrying about us leaving?"

"I know, I know. But two months doesn't sound long enough."

Even though we planned to spend most of our trip with the family, Maxx and I also wished to travel for a couple of weeks after the wedding. Just the two of us. There were a few places on Earth we wanted to see before going back to Rimall.

I wished we could stay longer, but I only got two months of vacation. And Maxx needed to go back to his work with the security team, too.

"You can come with us," I suggested.

"Leave Earth?" Mom gasped.

"Why not? Dad could take a leave of absence. And you're working part-time, anyway, now. You guys can come with us to Rimall for vacation. And if you like it there, you can move permanently when Dad retires a few years down the road."

"Oh, it sounds exciting. I'd love to be closer to you." She perked up.

"We'd be so close, just a few steps away, really. The compound isn't that big. But it's quiet and isolated. A huge difference after living in a big city. Maxx and I love it, though. Maybe you'll love it too? You can also travel if you get bored. The resorts on Rimall's moons are fantastic."

The more I spoke, the more the idea of them moving to Rimall made sense to me. It'd be great to have them close. I just hoped they'd love this idea, too.

Mom seemed interested.

"I'll have to talk with Dad, of course," she said. "But it'd be wonderful to be with you again. With both of you. Especially when a baby comes."

"A baby?" I almost tripped on the smooth pavement.

Mom glanced at me sideways. "You are planning to have a family one day, aren't you?" Concern moved her dark eyebrows closer together when she looked at Maxx's back as he walked ahead with my dad and our luggage. "Can he... um?"

"Oh yes, he can." I laughed to cover up the warmth flushing my face.

In my video calls and messages, I'd been open about Maxx, his origins, and our relationship. But I hadn't come that far as to discuss his reproductive system and capabilities. My mom, of course, didn't know that the genetic material for her future grandchild was already stored in my body, waiting for the moment I'd go off birth control to take over.

I wondered if she'd freak out if I told her that some high-tech alien cyborg parts lived in her daughter's body waiting for the opportune moment to impregnate her. It was best to wait for a better moment to mention stuff like that, though.

My dad turned around, gesturing excitedly at the largest taxi in line. "That one should fit all of us, right?"

"It should, honey." Mom hurried ahead to organize and supervise the loading of our bags.

I watched as the three of them got busy at the trunk of the vehicle, with Mom and Dad mostly getting in Maxx's way as he loaded our suitcases in, lifting three at a time. As if sensing my gaze, Maxx gave me a grin and a wink over his shoulder.

It was a good day. It promised to be an amazing visit. And our future looked better than ever. I smiled so wide, my mouth hurt, and mouthed to him, *"I love you."*

"I love you, too," his lips formed in reply.

I couldn't wait to spend the rest of my life with this man.

More in My Holiday Tails

What Makes an Alien a Dad?

Maya

"*Pooh Bear,*
I know it sucks, but I hope you'll understand. You're a smart, strong girl. That's why I loved you all these years..."

Loved?

Past tense?

My heart stuttered, and it took a moment for it to restart. Even then, it didn't seem to work all that well; my feet and hands went cold, blood rushing away from them.

What was this letter from Walter, my boyfriend, practically my fiancé, supposed to mean?

I was afraid to continue reading, but my eyes ran down the glowing dark-blue lines of text on the opaque screen of the tablet I'd received for my personal use upon arrival to the planet Neron five months ago.

"The truth is, these ten months have been hard..."

No one expected them to be easy. We'd talked about it a lot before I left Earth. Both Walter and I knew that my long absence might be challenging for our relationship. But it'd been a mutual decision.

I'd shared everything with Walter, including every piece of communication I'd received from Neron back then. My medical tests turned out to be the most promising out of hundreds of others, deeming my uterus the best place on Earth for the development of a Voranian baby.

Walter and I decided together that I should participate in the experimental study as the first human surrogate to implant the embryo of anonymous donors from the country of Voran located on Planet Neron.

For us, it'd be a great opportunity to earn the money Walter needed to open his store. And for Voranians, it offered new opportunities to become parents for the human-Voranian couples on Neron.

Historically, there were far more boys than girls born in Voran. It resulted in a ratio of about one woman to nine or ten men. In addition to their own families, Voranian women often used artificial insemination to help men other than their husbands to start a family as single fathers.

With the creation of the Earth-Neron Liaison Committee several years ago, a marriage agreement was signed. Human women could apply to become wives of Voranian men. Several happy marriages had formed since.

However, humans could not reproduce with Voranians. Our species turned out to be biologically incompatible for procreation.

The goal of the study I'd been selected for was to give human wives of Voranian men the chance to carry the babies of their husbands on their own with the help of a Voranian egg donor. If successful, the results of the studies would benefit everyone.

For the Voranian women, it meant they would have to go through fewer pregnancies. The embryos created with donor eggs and the sperm of a Voranian man married to a human woman would be implanted directly into his wife, allowing her to carry the pregnancy to term.

A win-win situation.

Unfortunately, after months or even years of extensive tests and research, I'd been deemed the only suitable human subject so far.

Voranians had been ecstatic to get their hands on me and my uterus. They couldn't force me to participate in the study, of course, but they'd made their offer as enticing as possible. I'd gotten an all-expense-paid trip to Voran, including the spaceship travel, accommodation, and whatever else I needed, provided it was approved by the head of the study, Professor Thormus. I'd also received a large payment before I'd even boarded the spaceship, and I had been promised five times as much upon the completion of the study.

This was supposed to be our new start, Walter's and mine. Nineteen to twenty months spent apart didn't seem too bad, considering we'd been together since we were sixteen—ten years now. We'd talked about getting married as soon as I got back to Earth, which would be only nine more months, including the five-month-long trip back.

The long-distance relationship hadn't been easy. We mostly communicated by written messages. Sending occasional videos was also allowed by my contract. We'd managed just fine. The study was more than half-way through already.

But now, this letter from Walter came...

"I feel like my life has been put on hold. I have a girlfriend who isn't here. Technically, I'm in a relationship, but I have to do everything alone. I feel out of place at both single and couple events. It sucks..."

Well, it sucked for me, too. But we were in it together. Except that I also had to go through our separation while carrying an alien fetus in my belly.

"Anyway, I hope you understand, Pooh Bear. I'm sorry, but I just can't go on like this..."

What?

What was that supposed to mean?

I got up from the small table on the rooftop terrace of the hospital building in Voran that had been my home since my arrival on Neron. My nose started to prickle from the inside, and my vision blurred. I blinked to clear the haze, but it barely helped.

The text on the tablet screen appeared to swim.

"I've been trying to figure out the best way to tell you, but it is what it is. I want to be single, Maya. Properly single, without having a girlfriend out there among the stars somewhere..."

A sob bubbled up my throat, and I threw a hand over my mouth.

The beautiful rooftop gardens weren't crowded, but there were people around. A few hospital technicians in white coveralls strolled along the mosaic stone paths. A couple were sitting on a bench two tables away from me, having lunch.

I tried to hide my face from view, hiding behind my dark, long hair.

Ten years... I'd been with Walter for ten years, and all it took for our relationship to fall apart was a few months spent away from each other.

"I hate to hurt you, Pooh Bear, but I have to be completely honest here. Maybe I just don't love you enough to go ahead with this commitment. Maybe I grew to love my single life too much. I never really had a chance to be single before..."

My next breath came rough and coarse. I hurried along the path. My chest tightened. Tears burned behind my eyelids, but I couldn't let them out in public.

How could he?

How could he do this to me when I'm millions of miles away from home? I was the only human in this entire hospital. As part of the study, I wasn't allowed to leave, to socialize, or to make friends with anyone outside of the premises.

Walter was my main connection to the outside world. And now, he was leaving me...

I sniffled, desperately trying to hold back my tears.

"Are you alright?" one of the technicians asked sympathetically while passing by.

His kindness undid me.

I nodded, hiding behind my hair, and almost sprinted around the tall hedge toward the exit. But I didn't make it. Tears ran down my face in a torrential stream. My knees gave out.

Two Voranian nurses appeared up ahead. The last thing I wanted was to cause a scene. I scrambled off the path and under the nearest tree. Crouching, I climbed into a bush with big yellow flowers and let the tears flow.

I felt so alone, like I was the only person in the entire Universe.

Kear

ON THE WAY FROM THE lab to his office, Kear made a detour to grab a lunch tray from the small café in the gardens on the roof of the hospital building.

Of course, he could have sent a drone to pick it up instead of walking three floors up only to go four floors down right after, but excitement buzzed through him, spurring him to move. The bounce in his step was so pronounced, he was practically dancing on his hooves.

On his way to the café, he went over the latest charts on his tablet. It looked good. Everything looked so fucking good, it was scary. Concerns could spring up unexpectedly with any pregnancy. But when it was the one-of-a-kind pregnancy in the entire Universe, everything was a risk.

The last five months had been the most intense in his life, which was significant, considering his life before hadn't always been easy, either. Yet this study proved more challenging than anything he'd done before.

Thankfully, the hard work seemed to be paying off. The subject's hormone levels were great. Her health seemed fine. The fetus's measurements were on the lower end of the scale but still within normal range. All organs looked perfect.

For the first time ever, a Voranian fetus was thriving in a human womb. It was a huge achievement. He couldn't wait to present his findings at the assembly this weekend. He could already imagine the envious looks on the faces of Hezer and Egus.

The three of them graduated from the academy together. Kear had been in the top of his class, but he'd taken a break right after to serve as a field doctor during the last two years of the war with the *fescods,* the semi-intelligent blob-like creatures that had taken over the nearby planet Tragul before invading the Voranian planet Neron. It had been the most brutal war in this part of the galaxy.

He'd learned a lot during his years on the battlefield and gained skills he would not have been able to gain anywhere else—like working without modern medical equipment, treating wounds with medicine sourced from local plants and animals, or thinking fast and taking risks that saved lives. It'd been a valuable experience, but it had set him back academically.

When he resumed his studies and his research work after the war, he had to catch up. Many of his colleagues had advanced far beyond him.

He got lucky, incredibly lucky, to stumble upon the breakthrough before anyone else. Since he was the one who'd found the subject with the best compatibility score, he had been appointed as the Head of Research during the most important study in the reproductive field yet.

Kear was only thirty-four—a ridiculously young age in the science world. Everything he'd achieved since his lucky break was through hard work, learning, and determination. Yet he found himself constantly having to defend his accomplishments in front of his much older and more experienced colleagues.

Well, at the assembly this weekend, he'd prove that the respect and honor he'd received from the nation was well earned on his part. The human subject of his study—

A strangled sob coming from the bushes beside the stone path made him pause. Tearing his attention away from his tablet screen, he lifted his head.

Another sob came—a squeaky, pitiful sound, followed by a sniffle. It appeared someone was crying. Only he couldn't see anyone around. Not that he knew what to do with a crying person, even if he saw them. The best he could think of would be getting a drone for assistance.

He lifted his tablet again, intending to call a hospital drone, when movement caught his eye. A foot in a white hospital shoe shifted on the ground, quickly disappearing under the nearest bush.

Voranians had hooves and wore no shoes. To his knowledge, there was currently only one pair of feet in this entire hospital. And it belonged to his study subject.

If she was the one crying, it was a problem, and it concerned him directly.

He lowered his tablet, staring at the dirt under the bush where the foot had just been. Another sob came from behind the flowers. This one was barely audible as she must've noticed him and covered her mouth with her hands, not wanting him to hear her crying.

Fuck, he didn't want to hear it either. If there was one thing that made him feel uncomfortably helpless, it was a crying woman. He had no idea what to do and wished he could just pretend he heard nothing, get his food, and eat it in peace in his office, like he'd intended.

But the human was crying. Which meant she was in distress. Which in turn meant her mental wellbeing was in jeopardy. Her physical wellbeing might also be at risk, and so were his perfect charts he was about to present at the biggest assembly in his field.

He couldn't let a drone handle this.

"Um..." He cleared his throat, speaking to the bush. "Madam..."

What was her name again? In all the research documents, she was referred to only by the subject number. Of course, he'd personally signed her immigration papers. He'd seen her full name listed there. But what was it? As great as his memory was at retaining large strings of research data, any irrelevant information didn't stay there for long.

"Madam." He decided to omit the name for now. "May I inquire what has caused your distress?"

The bush remained quiet; even the sobbing had ceased. Well, there was not much left to do. Crouching down, he set aside his tablet and parted the flower-covered branches.

She sat on the ground, hugging her knees as closely as her protruding belly allowed. The white cap she had worn during the physical exam that morning was gone. Her thick black hair was spread over her shoulders, with a few long tresses hanging over her face. Her dark eyes glistened as she glared at him through her thick, glossy strands.

"I'm fine."

She obviously lied. She looked the opposite of fine. The skin around her eyes was puffy. Her cheeks were flushed, making her appear feverish. Tears streaked her face.

Unease crawled up Kear's spine, urging him to flee. He felt way out of his element here. He'd much rather face a raging *fescod*. At least then, he'd know what to do. But he couldn't leave her like this. Her pulse must be racing. Her blood pressure was likely elevated. Neither would look good on his daily report charts.

"Can I take you to your apartment?" he asked.

Actually, he should take her back to the lab and take an entirely new set of data. Just to make sure nothing horrible was threatening his study subject.

Worry wormed into his chest.

"Are you hurt? Any cramping? Bleeding?"

His heart thumped in his chest at the last word. Risk factors could spring up during any pregnancy. And this one was so unique, even he didn't know exactly what to expect.

Misery eased from her expression. She made a visible effort to collect herself.

"No. Sorry, Professor Thormus. I didn't mean to scare you. I'm well. Just..." She sniffed again, glancing aside. "Just some things from back home... Nothing to worry about."

He noticed a tablet on the ground next to her. Irritation stirred in him. He had considered forbidding her all outside communications for the duration of the study, but Representative Alcus Hecear from the Voranian branch of the Liaison Committee convinced him that keeping in touch with the subject's loved ones would be good for her mental health.

Now, he could punch himself for agreeing with that. Any communication carried the risk of receiving bad news, and bad news never improved anyone's wellbeing.

"You can go, Professor Thormus." She waved at him. "I'll be fine. Promise."

The fact that she knew his name made him feel guilty about having forgotten hers. But then again, this clinic bore his name. It was on the signs on every floor and all official documentation. It made it much easier to remember.

Hers, on the other hand...

"Listen, Madam... Um."

She wiped the tears off her cheeks with the end of the hospital robe she was wearing over the examination gown. "Just Maya."

"Pardon me?"

"You can just call me Maya. It's my first name. You don't have to say Madam Gupta all the time."

He'd never said either. But at least now he had her name.

Maya.

It was short enough to remember.

She kept rubbing at her cheeks with her robe, sitting in the dirt of the flowerbed. He cringed at the thought of the germs she must've picked up by crawling around. Producing a pack of sanitizing wipes from his pocket, he handed her one.

"Here. It's gentle enough to use on your face." He pulled out another one. "And this one is for your hands."

"Thanks." She took the wipes, cleaned her face and hands, then blew her nose.

With all those tears running for who knew how long, she must be dehydrated. She likely hadn't had lunch yet either if she'd been sitting here since her morning exam.

"When was the last time you ate?"

She balled up the wipes and stuffed them into the pocket of her robe.

"I'm not hungry."

Hunger had nothing to do with it. She required a steady flow of nutrition to ensure an optimal environment for the fetus. Skipping meals was unacceptable and against the rules outlined in the contract.

"Come. I'll get you lunch." He climbed to his hooves.

There was a smudge on the left pant leg of his coverall. The dirt from the flower bed must have gotten on it somehow, despite his best efforts to avoid it. He winced at the sight of the dark-brown stain on the crisp white fabric. But there were infinitely more stains on the human's clothes. He had to get her out of those bushes.

"Come on." He offered her a hand.

"I'd rather stay here," she said softly. Her bottom lip trembled. She looked utterly miserable once again.

He rubbed his forehead, trying to figure out what to do about this situation.

"Should I call Alcus Hecear?"

Representative Alcus Hecear was everything Kear was not—smiling, diplomatic, tactful, a people person in every way. As the Head of the Liaison Committee, Alcus was involved in dealing with any problems occurring in human-Voranian relationships. Humans loved him. Voranians respected him. He would know how to coax Maya out of this bush.

Kear turned on his tablet, ready to request Alcus's contact.

"No. Don't." She sighed. "I don't want to make a scene. It's not a big deal." Getting on all fours, she finally crawled out of the bushes, then retrieved her tablet. "I'll just go back to my apartment now."

He couldn't let her out of his sight, not while she looked so miserable, like an *ulto* pup pulled out of water.

"Why don't you have lunch with me?" He blinked in shock at his own proposition.

He always ate alone, unless it couldn't be helped, like during formal meetings or official functions. He certainly didn't remember ever inviting anyone to share a meal before. But he couldn't trust his subject to eat something nutritious if he allowed her to return to her apartment on her own. He suspected she'd just cry again and miss lunch completely. It was best to feed her where he could supervise her food intake.

"What's your favorite Voranian food?" he asked. "Today, I'll allow you to have whatever you like on top of your pre-planned meal."

"Really?" Her smile was sad and rather pitiful, but it was so much better than tears. "Anything I like? Even if it's not on the list of approved stuff?"

He hesitated. The list was there for a reason. He'd personally compiled it, matching human ingredients to Voranian ones to ensure a proper mix of nutrients for her.

"Is there something you'd like outside of that list?" he asked tentatively.

"*Ice cream,*" she replied way too quickly. She'd clearly had it in mind for some time now. "Or whatever closest substitute you have for it in Voran. Frozen cream with sugar, chocolate, and caramel sauce."

His translator implant fired off the Voranian substitutes of the ingredients she'd listed. None of them were on the list of the approved foods, because all of them would wreak havoc on her system.

He stared at her in horror. The woman was a menace to herself.

"How about some frozen cultured milk with fruit juice and berries instead?" he suggested. She made a face, and he added quickly, "That's as close a substitute as you'll get in my clinic."

She dropped her shoulders and silently followed him to the order counter of the rooftop café as if he were leading her to an execution.

Why did it bother him so much to see her upset?

"Fine." He pinched the bridge of his nose. "I'll let them sweeten it."

She perked up, glancing at the order screen from around his bicep. "You'll add sugar?"

Absolutely not.

"A tree nectar from the planet Tragul," he named a much healthier alternative to the sweetener that she referred to. "It contains traces of several useful nutrients, at least."

"But what does it taste like?"

"Like flowers. You'll like it."

AVAILABLE NOW

More by Marina Simcoe

The World of the River of Mists

Joyless Kingdom (Trilogy)
Somber Prince, Book 1
Joy Guardian, Book 2
Pleasure Trader, Book 3

Wingless Crow (Duet)
Wingless Crow – Part 1
Crownless King – Part 2

Fire in Stone (Duet)
Fire in Stone – Part 1
Hearts on Fire – Part 2

Serpent's Touch (Duet)
Serpent's Touch – Part 1
Serpent's Claim – Part 2

Madame Tan's Freakshow (Trilogy)

Call of Water
Madness of the Moon
Power of Rage

Paranormal Romance

About the Author

Marina Simcoe likes to write love stories with characters, who may or may not be entirely human, because she firmly believes that our contemporary world could always use a little bit of the extraordinary.

She has lots of fun exploring how her out-of-this-world characters with their own beliefs, values, and aspirations fit into our every-day life.

She lives in Canada with her very own grumpy brute, their three little kids, and a cat, who is definitely out of this world.

For the illustrations to this and other books by the author, please join her Patreon:

Please Stay in Touch

Newsletter signup is on MarinaSimcoe.com:

Facebook Readers' Group:
Marina's Reading Cave
www.instagram.com/marinasimcoeauthor
www.marinasimcoe.com
www.facebook.com/MarinaSimcoeAuthor/
www.amazon.com/author/marinasimcoe
www.bookbub.com/profile/marina-simcoe
www.goodreads.com/MarinaSimcoe

www.ingramcontent.com/pod-product-compliance
Lightning Source LLC
Chambersburg PA
CBHW061349310726